# The Children's Horror

## Cursed Episodes for Doomed Adults

### Patrick Barb

NORTHERN REPUBLIC

*The Secret Society of Schrödinger's Children* originally appeared in *Cosmic Horror Monthly*.

*The Shark in Her Belly* originally appeared in Dark Recesses Webzine.

*Rat Suit King* originally appeared in *Chthonic Matter Quarterly*.

All other stories are original to this collection.

Book Cover by Paul Stephenson @ Hollow Stone Press.

To Grant and Avery, watching you discover the joys of storytelling is
one of my favorite parts of this gig.

# Contents

# FOREWARNING

Ever hear of Captain Midnight?

In 1986, HBO had its signal feed hacked. If you lived in the eastern half of the United States and were hoping to watch *The Falcon and the Snowman* that evening—whelp—you were shit out of luck, subjected instead to a color-barred protest over high subscription fees for nearly five bewildering minutes.

What about the Max Headroom signal hijacking back in 1987? A pirated broadcast of a man wearing a mask beamed its way across Chicago's airwaves for seventeen seconds.

Then, it happened again. Our rubber-masked Max came back later that same night, this time for a total of ninety seconds, interrupting none other than Dr. Who. With a stronger signal, Max become bolder in its pirated presentation, tossing cans of New Coke in the air and getting spanked on his bare bottom with a fly swatter by another cloaked individual.

Ninety seconds. To this day, nobody knows who donned the Max Headroom mask.

Broadcast signal intrusions, rare as they are, happen. Talk about timing. It's the ultimate "you just had to be there" occurrence. Just imagine: you're at home, watching TV, when all of a sudden the images distort. The sound crackles. Your regularly scheduled programming is disrupted and you are exposed to a lo-fi, static-laced broadcast, abruptly thrust out of the comfort zone of your couch and into the analogue ramblings of madmen.

Were you lucky enough to be watching? Did you see what happened?

Were you turned on and tuned in when it occurred?

Personally, I have never experienced a broadcast signal intrusion. Not in real time, at least. They are out there, ready and desperate to be found on YouTube, but I have always coveted the disruptive experience of a pirated signal jolting me out of my status quo.

This is the stuff of Reddit obsessives. Dig around the internet and you will find clips that have built the sturdy foundation for creepypastas and online urban legends in abundance.

But were you really there? Did you see it for yourself? With your own eyes?

Now that we are deep into the era of streamers, I can feel the opportunity slipping even further and further away from me. What other than awards shows and Super Bowls demands that audiences tune in now? At this very moment? The real-time quality of a transmission is fading, replaced by the algorithmic clicks of Netflix, Amazon, and beyond.

Then, I read *The Children's Horror*.

Patrick Barb is broadcasting his own signal intrusion. The stories in this collection exist in a parallel dimension, hewing so close to our own regularly scheduled programming and yet... not. It is the uncanny valley of children's shows. Cartoons and nature programs that feel so eerily familiar, so strangely similar to the programming pap that dominates our own children's screentime, you will swear—swear—you've seen them before. Haven't you?

What kind of déjà vu is this?

I go back to that Max Headroom mask. The hacked broadcast. It's meant to represent the iconic character that a whole generation of television viewers know so well.

It's him. From the commercials. But at the same time… it's not.

It's a façade. An intruder in a rubber facsimile, clearly not the real thing.

That's what makes it so scary.

It's Max… but not.

It's TV… but not.

Patrick Barb is offering us up glimpses of children's television programming that we have all experienced on some level, either as viewers ourselves or as parents in need of a reprieve from our own children, saddling them up with their tablets to give us a break.

A part of me wants to say this book was written explicitly for parents. As one, I've already been subjected to the horror—some might say torture—of watching a lot of the original programming that serves as inspiration for the stories you are about to read here.

I don't want to tell you how many times I've listened to the "Baby Shark" song. Countless times. An infinite amount. It's still playing in my head at this very moment, rattling about my brain, an earworm gleefully echoing throughout my skull. I have listened to that goddamn song more than any other song I've ever listened to, more than any one man should ever be subjected to. It is torture. Absolute torture. The tune was on an endless loop in our household for months, cycling through our tablets until we had to say stop.

But it never really stops, does it? Not in Patrick Barb's world.

Which means not for you, either.

I've had the good fortune of meeting Patrick Barb in person. We've hung out at literary events. Were this not the case, and I'd simply been giving this book to read… I might not believe Patrick Barb was, in fact, a real person. I might say he's the man hiding behind the Max Headroom mask, forcing his way onto the airwaves and into my mind.

He is the signal intrusion.

If you're ever in Patrick Barb's presence and you squint from a distance, something about his visual demeanor leaves him looking a bit like a youngish Captain Kangaroo.

Makes sense, if you think about it. I'm thinking about it all the time, now that I've read *The Children's Horror*. Patrick Barb is more than just an author. He's the host with the most. *The Children's Horror* is his own show. On its surface, it's meant for children—of a certain generation, perhaps, but children all the same—his target audience wide-eyed and innocent, uncorrupted by the curdled programming contained in these pages. Much like Mr. Rogers or Bozo the Clown, there's a call-and-response with his live audience. A price to pay. What exactly is that toll? It's not my place to say… Not yet, at least.

Let's talk after you've finished this collection of stunning stories, okay?

Because let's be honest with ourselves here… You don't just watch *The Children's Horror*. *The Children's Horror* watches you back.

And it wants in.

Clay McLeod Chapman
*July 2024*

# THE CHILDREN'S HORROR

The children's horror is a certain, solid thing waiting in the dark. Our preparations to leave the school take time, as we have to make sure to stay clear of shadows. Especially when the sun's moved higher in the sky, its long rays acting like fertilizer for the outstretched shades extending from our bodies and from every object around us. Ms. Nina holds the backdoor open, letting purifying sunlight into the hallway, shining back on the classrooms. Watercolor portraits of the children's pets, siblings, and other loved ones remain taped to the wall outside her room. My class hung Crayola-colored maps of the United States. A rainbow of hues for all fifty states. One of the kids—a little boy, Ryan—colored the Atlantic and Pacific Oceans in oranges and reds.

When he handed me the picture to hang on the wall, I asked, "Why'd you choose those colors for the ocean?" At the time, I wore a natural smile, not forced in the slightest.

"It's the river of Hell," the boy said. He was clear-eyed and the words came from his mouth without a stutter or lisp or any of the other affectations children possess at that age. Listening to a first-grader speak of "the river of Hell" was more offensive than if he'd dropped an f-bomb or tried to grab my breast. There was something adult in his pronunciation. No, not adult. *Ancient.* Like something existing beyond the boy with a rat-tail and me, his teacher. Something beyond Sunny Rivers Elementary School. Beyond life on Earth itself.

"Aida, come on," Miss Nina says, standing with one leg under the flickering fluorescent tube lighting overhead and her other in the burnt umber sunlight. She's split in two under this dual illumination. Two separate halves of two separate people shoved together.

I hesitate.

"Are you sure none of them touched you?" I ask. I hate the way my voice sounds, too soft and scared. Ms. Nina's seen as much of the horror as I have, but she's kept her "teacher" voice—strong, soothing.

Her smooth palm has turned skeleton-white with chalk dust. "I swear."

I look back through the rectangular glass window on the closed door of my classroom. Somehow not quite ready to leave *them*.

***

Before the children's horror, circle time was informed by whispers. First from the back of the group, one girl in pigtails leaning to the side with her lips too close to the earlobe of another wearing rainbow barrettes. Pop-Tart crumbs from breakfast gave form to whatever secrets the pigtail girl shared willingly.

Even as I went through the motions, asking the children to tell me what day of the week and selecting a volunteer to place a laminated sun or storm cloud with a cartoon face on the "weatherboard," I watched these secrets spread from one child sitting crisscross applesauce to the next.

When circle time ended, every child must've received the new good word. From my vantage point, it seemed they'd undergone a religious experience. Their eyes rolled back white. Every single tiny person sitting around me showed eyes the tint and rheumy texture of soft-boiled eggs. I set my felt board down, letting the limp cut-out figures of Goldilocks and the Three Bears drift to the carpet.

"Children?" I asked, addressing them as one. Not yet grasping how close to the truth this was.

"Yes, Miss Aida," one of the girls, her hair black and brushed out high like storm clouds, answered. Darla was her name. *Is* her name.

"Is something wrong, Darla? With you and..." I waved my hand, indicating the whole class with the sweep of my arm.

The children, despite the sickly white appearance of their eyes, followed my movement. Like dogs watching their master's hand with a treat. And like the dogs, an unspoken menace resided in the way they tracked me. The suggestion being, if those dogs wanted, they could *take* the treat and their master's hand with it.

"No, Miss Aida."

This time a boy answered, Jaxon H., the most memorable of the four boys named Jaxon in my class. Jaxon H.'s dad owned a liquor store, a sporting goods store, an air-conditioning repair service, or something. It made him enough of a town bigshot so people in the front office and teacher's lounge took note when I had his son enrolled in my class.

The children kept looking at me, even though it didn't appear that they were *looking* at me. In addition to their rolled-back eyes, they held their faces in a certain way, something beyond daydreaming. Their active, ever-evolving features were kept in check, as though flash-frozen. I pulled my legs from under my bottom and stood, too quickly and more than a little unevenly. Pain shot through my thighs and calves. A dull tingling followed. As though my legs had fallen asleep.

I steadied myself on the silvered edge of the chalkboard, then glanced at the clock. The numbers showed huge on the clock face for when the kids had their unit on telling time, so there was no mistaking what I saw. Barely ten minutes had passed since we'd started circle-time and the children had begun...changing.

All in less than ten minutes.

At least as far as my perception of the change was concerned...

*But that realization came later in the school day.*

I straightened my skirt against my legs, rubbing my limbs harder than I might normally in front of the children. It wouldn't do for their teacher to flop on the floor like a fish pulled from the water though.

They remained seated. Something they never, ever did. The slightest squeaky fart from a quiet girl or an unexpected announcement from Principal Ward over the loudspeaker used to send my little guys and gals into tittering hysterics.

But not the day of the children's horror.

*We want to show you what we're making...*

The voice sounded like one of my children. I mean I'd had my little ones for six months, so I knew all of their sweet voices by then. But looking at them, with their necks all tilted back like loosened Pez dispensers, blank features directed at me, I couldn't pick out a single pair of moving lips.

And the voice—it was Ryan. It was Darla. It was Jaxon H. No, Jaxon C., or W., or the other C. It was Madeline, Charles, Georgie, Georgina, Rebecca, Molly, Jennifer... It was all of them at once.

And none of them.

The ringing of the intra-classroom telephone provided a shrill, shrieking lifeline, pulling me free from murky uncertainty. I forced myself free from the children's blank, immobile faces and walked across the room to grab the tan corded phone hung by the coat closet.

I picked up the receiver and pressed it to my ear. The cool touch of molded plastic offered a momentary soothing. I hadn't understood how hot I was. But a glance revealed sweat-soaked, already yellowing armpits on my short-sleeved white blouse top.

"Hello?"

"How're your children?"

Ms. Nina. My relief at her voice was unlike anything I'd experienced. Like I'd run a marathon and come crashing across the finish line, ready for the tinfoil blanket, water, and rub-downs.

It must've manifested in a sigh or sharp intake of breath or something because Ms. Nina chuckled on the other end of the line. "That good, huh?"

Ms. Nina talked to her fellow teachers like some wily veteran police officer or front-line soldier, providing gallows humor to go with her homespun wisdom.

I found myself turning further from the children and their circle. Once I faced the classroom door, I let the cord wrap around my arm like a malnourished snake. I cupped a hand over the speaker before I spoke again. "Things're a tad *different* this morning."

"You're goddamn right!"

I gasped. "Ms. Nina!"

Sure, there was a time and a place for a potty mouth. But Ms. Nina had her kids in circle time as well. Same as all of us teachers on the hall. We all shared similar lesson plans.

It didn't seem right to curse in front of the children.

"Oh, don't worry," she said. "My kids have gone."

"Where—"

"Some walked out of the classroom, right out the door. A few others went into the class bathroom and jimmied themselves up into the vents. You'll catch 'em rattling around up there if you listen long enough."

As if on cue, a loud bang sounded above me. Like the report of a pistol or a tiny pair of Keds kicking the interior of the air conditioning vents in our old building.

"Have you talked to any of the other teachers…"

"No, doll," Ms. Nina said in a way that reminded me of Paul Newman, leaning against a brick wall with a toothpick balanced on his perfect teeth. "I tried every class on our hallway. Nobody else is home."

"D-d-do you wanna come here?" I asked. I pressed my forehead against the window above the door. We'd placed shredded cotton ball pieces on the glass aiming for a hopeful message, encouraging the children to *reach for the sky*.

"How many of them you got in there?"

I knew what she was referring to. *Who* she was referring to. I turned slow and steady, letting my flats grind against the crayon-encrusted carpet. I got set to give her a number. I figured something like fifteen. Twenty-two if everyone showed up for school on the day and it appeared that everyone *was* present, the way they'd crowded around me before. "Oh there's…"

*One.*

One child stood behind me, waiting for me to finish my call and return my attention to them. I looked around, trying to determine if I could spot a wayward sneaker or rainbow bubblegum barrette, hear giggling and whispers, or find some other tell-tale sign of children hiding and doing a terrible job of it.

But there was nothing. There was only the child, soft-cheeked, short-haired. Eyes rolled back white, lips moist and parted to reveal tiny Chicklet-sized teeth. The skin was a mottled mash of flavors, skin tones bubbling under the surface like the bulbous excretions in a lava lamp.

The child was all of the children in my class. But also none of them. Its voice sounded in my head again.

*"I/we are the Children's Horror…"*

Ms. Nina opened the door to my classroom and pulled me into the hallway. I held back the vomit long enough so it sprayed the cotton ball clouds on the door and dripped down the glass and polished teak.

Pressed against the opposite wall, I watched my sick inching down the door before it splattered onto the ground. The Children's Horror met my fevered gaze, stretching up to press its elongated face against the glass. As it grinned at us, one face, two faces, all of my children's faces appeared tiny and red, like some outbreak of acne across its composite face. These tiny faces, like pustules, grew bigger, bigger, bigger, and then…*POP!*

***

Too traumatized to absorb the empty, silent hallways and the too-easy retreat we'd made, Ms. Nina and I barricaded ourselves in the teacher's lounge, pushing the plaid pattern couch and chair against the door. The furniture looked like something out of my parents' basement and stank of it too. Fabric soaked with cigarette smoke so you'd convince yourself your hands would come away nicotine-yellow just from being near it.

Ms. Nina put her hand on my cheek, a softer touch than she'd provided in the hallway where she'd back-handed the incoherent screams out of me. She'd hit me so hard it'd opened up a cut on my cheek. Blood still dribbled onto my blouse.

"Sorry, hon." Ms. Nina switched to her teacher's voice once we'd settled in the lounge. Like she needed some child to teach, but instead, had to settle for me—her younger colleague. I didn't fight though. There was a comfort to it.

"What're we going to do?" I asked.

In response, she held up the black phone hanging beside the staff fridge. "Could try this again. But last few times I missed a dial-tone."

I didn't dare ask what she'd heard instead. As it stood, my lip was trembling and I wanted it to stop. I wanted to cope with the end of the world—because that's damn sure what it felt like—with the same relaxed nonchalance as Ms. Nina.

She raised her eyebrow like she'd read my mind and was now worried I'd crack under the pressure. I lowered my gaze and took in her hand, puffy and red from where she'd struck me earlier. She turned and opened the fridge door, letting its pale yellow glow out into the lounge.

She pulled out sack lunch after sack lunch, each belonging to one of our missing colleagues.

Ms. Nina pulled about five bags before she said, "Well, you wanna help or what? Let's check what we can eat here. Or save for later..."

"O-o-okay..."

I moved to the fridge.

The crackle of the intercom stopped me in my tracks. Ms. Nina straightened at the sound, closing the fridge at the same time. I caught a glimpse of the light before it blinked away. I swore I glimpsed the afterimage of eyes glowing from somewhere past the egg salads and the janitor's leftover birthday cake as the door slammed close.

"Attention! Boys, girls, and teachers...will everyone please come to the auditorium for a special treat..."

It was our principal, Stan Gilhooley. The older kids called him the Gil-Monster. He was one of those disciplinarian types. Real ball-buster, even at the elementary level. Hearing the words, "special treat" spoken by Principal Gilhooley should've told us something was amiss right away. Hell, hearing him refer to the children as "boys and girls" and not "students," didn't sit right either.

Ms. Nina must've felt the same. She crossed her arms over her chest and glared at the intercom tucked away in the corner by the ceiling like she'd glanced up and found a wasp's nest hanging there defiant. "Well...what is it?" she asked, speaking as though Gilhooley stood in the room with us.

"Uh-uh, you've gotta come to the auditorium. No spoiling our...my...surprise..."

"Children?" I asked without thinking, bringing my hand to my mouth as though I could force the word back.

Another pause on the intercom, then the loud whine of feedback masked the moans and demoniac cries of the damned. When Principal Gilhooley spoke again, he sounded like a defeated, broken man. And we soon learned how broken.

"Oh God...they took...my head. My head! Why'm I still alive? Why? Let me die again. Why do I feel...everything? They've got their...little...devil's hands...moving my mouth...eyes...They're pulling...I'm not a puppet!"

Loud, phlegmy choking followed. Then, the falsely cheerful children's version of Gilhooley's voice regained control. "Whoopsy-doopsy," he/they said. "Come on, ladies, don't make me come in there and draggggggggg you out..."

The tiny quarter-inch-sized holes on the intercom speaker filled with a pale pink substance. Like looking at a pointillist painting, I had to step back from the dots to understand what we were being shown. But as flesh, blood, and malleable bone leaked through along with eyes, teeth, and tongue...we understood.

There was Principal Gilhooley making good on his promise to come and get us. "The children's horror..." Ms. Nina said, while our boss's mincemeat head dribbled to the floor.

"This isn't possible," I said. Not because I believed it, but because I wished more than anything that what I said *was* true. I wanted my eyes to open, a feverish chill passing through my body. I wanted this to all be a dream—a nightmare. Hell, I'd settle for it being a final distorted vision on my deathbed. Some explanations making some rational sense.

But the quivering lumps of flesh at our feet, reaching for each other and growing each time they touched, told a different story, giving reasons beyond reason.

A knocking on the door followed. I looked at Ms. Nina and she looked back at me. She shrugged like *What're you gonna do, kid?*

I let her take my hand and lead me to the teacher's lounge door. We pulled away the furniture blocking our way. Then, she turned the knob and pulled open the door, exposing us to whatever waited in the hall.

No one.

No one waited for us.

We headed to the auditorium all the same. Because we didn't know where else to go.

***

The children—my children, Ms. Nina's, and the other classes' children—filled the seats in the old auditorium. So many tiny faces and tiny bodies filled the folded-down theater chairs in row after row. Their legs kicked the air, coming up shy of the seatbacks ahead. When the double doors leading into the theater space slammed behind us, we peered through the darkness, examining rows lit by the track lighting on the floor. The children's too-big chairs creaked and whined, as their bodies wriggled to hold the seats down.

Ms. Nina and I made our way to the main aisle. We kept our eyes straight ahead. I didn't want to look to the side and catch a glimpse of one of my children. I didn't want to watch their faces melting or bubbling or—maybe worse—not changed at all, but accepting of the madness in which we'd landed.

A gray and black TV cart sat on the lip of the stage, centered so the audience got a decent view of whatever appeared on the screen no matter where they sat. The TV resting atop the cart with a black luggage strap keeping it in place was one of those huge 1980s Magnavox sets. A beast of a machine with a greyed-out screen as thick as a block of ice. A set you could drop on someone's head and make a real mess of them in doing so.

The TV was off with the power light presenting a dull autumnal orange. We stopped at the front row, shy of the stage. No one made a sound behind or around us. Then, the children spoke to us telepathically. A chorus of cherubic voices in our heads again.

*We need you to turn on our shows.*

On testing days, we'd bring the kids into the auditorium and play cartoons for them. Nothing with any real educational value. No *Sesame Street* or *Mr. Rogers*, but the usual Saturday morning and after-school dreck. Gilhooley hated it, but we always fought to preserve this twice-annual respite for our kids. "They work so hard," one of us would always say, "Don't they deserve a break? Some fun?"

Gilhooley would grunt and wave us off. Never offering his *true* opinion, but not willing to put up a fight either.

Ms. Nina dropped my hand and left me on the floor. She walked up the steps and onto the stage. Her hand reached for the power knob. She twisted it.

"Ow!"

She pulled her hand back, then brought fingertips to her lips. Like she'd gotten stung. Or stabbed.

When she returned to the front of the stage, she took my hand again and led me to the empty row in the back. We sat behind the children, settling into our seats and finding them the right fit—maybe even a little too snug.

I looked at Ms. Nina's hand, her fingertip bleeding onto the mahogany armrest. "You okay?" I whispered.

*Shhhhhhhhhhhhhhhh!*

The children's psychic shushing echoed like a raging hurricane in my skull. My eyes watered as my eardrums throbbed, ripe enough to burst.

Ms. Nina shook her head. Like I'd disappointed her. Like I'd misunderstood something fundamental that'd make all the difference in the outcome of our day. My cheeks flushed red and I turned back to the stage.

The TV's glow cast a blanket of soft light across the front rows of the audience. The children stared in awe at the machine. An image appeared on-screen, something familiar. But different than what I remembered from my childhood and the glimpses my students gave me of their television favorites.

And then, the shows played.

NOT THE END...

# The Final Choice of Peter Chu

*"You're no freer than us, Peter Chu."*

I folded, unfolded, then re-folded the narrow slip of paper with the message scrawled in close-to-indecipherable handwriting. Even as I hid the scribblings from sight, their message hung before me, glowing with a searing intensity. They reminded me of the fiery holo-banners stretched across the arenas during my competition days.

My memories of the fighting pits always hit me hard. I reached for the orb floating near my hand. The metallic surface gave at my touch, allowing me to access the portable pocket dimension inside. I pictured what I wanted and let my fingers close around the object. When I pulled my hand out, the medicine dropper rested in my palm—refilled and waiting for use. One, two drops of amber liquid in each eye. When the solution hit the enlarged void of my pupils, they receded—returning to a normal *human* level.

"Whatcha got there, Pete?"

Kash's voice, always so full of enthusiasm, caught me by surprise. After all, I'd locked my doors. But Kash owned the building—so, of course, he had keys. *Of course.*

I made a fist around the dropper, reaching into my pocket to extract the folded note. I crammed both into my orb, leaving me with empty hands.

I fixed my shirt collar, and turned to face Kash Atkins. I maintained direct eye contact, not daring to look away from a man who dressed far too young for his age, but pulled it off through sheer force of will. "Fixing my eyes," I answered.

I turned my head, presenting a rounded cheek—once a perfect circle but stretched to a more oval shape thanks to one of many expensive procedures I'd undergone. Kash stood on tip-toes to kiss the offered cheek. A quick, cold peck between reunited friends.

The message was loud and clear. This was a business call.

Too little, too late, I scrambled to push aside unwelcome memories. In my reflection across the sphere, I watched my sallow skin flush bright crimson.

Kash chuckled.

"My friend, what's the matter? I come at a bad time?"

I wanted to berate him for strolling into my home—*my* home—as though the notion of private property, of a space of one's own, meant less than nothing. But an already growing sense of unease settled onto my weary shoulders, quieting me for the moment.

I shook my head. *No.* After multi-hour vocal cord surgeries meant to deepen intonations and allow for a full range of vocabulary, I still preferred silence or pantomime.

Kash barreled ahead, either not suspecting what impact his presence had...or not caring. "They've sighted the last one I need. Near Crater

Village of all places. Can you believe that? All the time spent searching, capturing so many, battling in arenas to claim others as spoils of victory...and the last one I need's waiting back home of all places. Pretty wild. Huh, buddy?"

*Buddy.* Like he called me before I changed. *Buddy.* Like he whispered as we camped under the stars that last night on the road. On the hunt.

*"Come here, buddy. Let's warm each other up"* Kash's breath reeking of the cheap sake that warmed our bellies, making my heart beat fast...faster...

Again, I caught my reflection warped in the orb's shiny, silver surface. I considered the man I'd become since my days with Kash. Metallic tubing, bolted and braced in place, stretched skin and muscle under my facial features producing the approximation of a neck. Limbs, broken and re-set, were pumped full of growth hormone to increase their size and provide more definition. Every morning, I endured a gauntlet of injections to ensure nothing atrophied. One slip-up, one moment of forgetfulness and I'd shrivel like a wilting balloon in a muggy basement.

I raised my gaze to Kash once more. My old companion was waiting, primed like a madman's bomb, set to go off when least expected. Always the man-child, a wispy mustache threatened mutiny against his smooth near-ivory skin. He wore a shit-eating grin without a parachute.

Even as he entered middle age, Kash still leapt into danger, trusting in whatever higher power provided him with his success to see him safe and sound to a final destination. His rehearsed and focus-group-tested expression made him more than Kash the poor boy from Crater Village who left home with a dream and not much else.

It made him *Kash Atkins: Hunter of Tiny Monsters, or TiMos for those in the know.* World-famous. The man with everything.

Well, *almost* everything.

I weighed each word before speaking them aloud. "Good," I said, "I wish you luck in your hunt."

"Oh, come on. Don't."

Kash took my hand in his, tracing a fingertip over the scar tissue in the spots where surgeons removed the webbing between my original three-digited appendage.

"Come," he said.

"No, Kash. Please."

"I need you. You're my lucky charm. You're my first and I want you there when I capture my last."

A spark, a crackle of electrical energy built in the pit of my stomach—my nerves and anxiety given physical form. Forever fighting an internal battle between what I once was and who I'd become, I gritted shaved-down teeth and blew out rapid-fire breaths from my reconstructed nostrils. I used every calming technique in my arsenal to repress the previous side of my nature and nurture the man I claimed to be. In the end, I reduced the sudden electric flare-up to a brief lightning flash across my already darkening eyes.

"First *what*, Kash? Last *what*?"

He took a step back, then another. Recognition of my discomfort settled over him. He tipped his dusty, worn baseball cap. When he spoke again, his voice was low. All business in a world of nothing but bad business. "You know, I don't have to *ask*, right?"

My mouth hung open, loosened like an abandoned ventriloquist's dummy jaw. Kash waited, not smiling, not rubbing it in. But displaying no outward signs of sorrow or regret either. A battle of wills played through this silence, and I knew how those always ended for the two of us.

I was left with no choice but to say, "Fine. I'll come."

A reinvigorated grin spread across Kash's face like a flesh-eating virus. I swallowed back my revulsion and the still-growing sense of fear for my safety, holding it in check long enough to return a forced smile of my own.

"But I won't fight for you," I said.

Kash nodded, already heading for the door, the transaction over once he got what he wanted. "Of course, of course. I know you're well past the old days. I'd never ask you to go against your nature."

"When do we leave?"

"As soon as possible," he answered.

*** 

Kash swerved across the dirt roads outside his home village. Brown leather driving gloves rubbed the mud-splattered steering wheel as he drove over every bump in our path. I stole a glance to the side, observing palm trees heavy with exotic fruit hiding thatched roof dwellings belonging to those who lived even further off the grid than the residents of Kash's Crater Town. Wild TiMo eyes of varied hues, reflecting the sinking late afternoon sunlight from various heights, stared back at me.

My orb floated beside our speeding vehicle, keeping pace with Kash's manic driving. Kash's orb lagged behind, coming like a stalking presence whenever I glanced at the rear-view mirror.

"Looks like ya got a lot on your mind, buddy!

He shouted over the roar of his belching diesel engine. Again, with the *buddy*. Again, with his hand on the gear shift, knuckles brushing my corduroy-covered leg.

Another awkward silence fell between us. Kash shrugged, acting like he'd shouted into a long, dark empty tunnel, not expecting to find any signs of life outside his echo bouncing back. We continued down the road in silence. The long dirt highway around Crater Town was a once primitive footpath widened to accommodate semi-modern vehicles, but no other changes were made. It reminded me of the treadmill track at the TiMo gym.

*"C'mon buddy. One more lap before your next match!"*

Instead of squeezing my eyes shut to banish another unwanted vision of the past, I forced them open wider. Kicked-up road dirt hit the corners of my re-touched eyelids. Tears streamed down cheeks whose yellow coloring intensified. I'd missed my monthly skin-dyeing appointment for this final hunt. The pink hue of my *human* cheeks faded like photographs on rotting newsprint.

The surface of Kash's orb cast an oil-spill pattern of light, like paint swirling down a drain. Round and round. Flashing, sparking, reds, yellows, blues, and greens, forming a mesmeric pattern

My eyes blinked in time with the signal. Old instincts triggered. I'd follow the rapid-fire pattern of an opponent's power moves in order to gauge the perfect moment to strike or block...or go for a knock-out blow.

All I wanted was to sever this tie to my old life. But unlike my physical appearance, the lived experience wasn't erased under the sharp touch of a surgeon's knife.

Past the swirl of reflected colors, I glimpsed something pure ebony in coloring. A creature with sleek, perfectly-formed limbs. It was a snatched sighting of night come early and poured into the form of a single ideal being.

*Wem.*

"Stop!" I shouted.

Kash's foot slammed on the brake. Dirt and rocks sprayed back across the long divots dug by the Jeep's tires. Kash's hat flew off his head, striking the steering wheel, then crashing to the wheel well. I made a quick note of the bald spot on the back of his head. Any other time, I'd savor the moment—catching sight of a rare imperfection. When he turned to me, I saw my smiling face reflected in his eyes. "I saw Wem," I told him.

***

We searched the jungle along the roadside, never venturing too far into the foliage. When darkness settled, even Kash conceded there was little hope of finding the ebon-tinted creature, without taking the time to prepare the proper equipment. We returned to our vehicle and finished the journey to a lodge on the outskirts of Crater Town.

On the plane ride up from the bustling metropolitan Bigg City, I asked Kash about staying with his family, since I knew a few members of the Atkins Clan had remained in the old village. But he struck down my line of questioning, waving his hand in a noncommittal fashion. The Kash Atkins sitting across from me was no longer Kash from Crater Town, no more than I, Peter Chu, was...*what I used to be.*

The lodge proved a shabby rustic affair—where *rustic* performed the heavy lifting for a more accurate descriptor of *shithole*. Rather than bother with check-in or waking up a sleeping bell clerk drooling onto his hand and the burnished silver bell of the countertop, we sauntered, bone-weary, over to the plywood-sheet-constructed bar, behind which sat a cooler full of beers. The lodge's seeming proprietor, a brassy woman with sunburnt cleavage the color of tomato skin, twisted bottles open with callused hands like cellophane-wrapped meat.

The exhaustion of travel and an impromptu Wem search caused me to forget about Crater Town's raised elevation and thinner air. After fewer beers than I care to admit, my human façade began to slip and tiny lighting strikes escaped with every belch.

Kash lived up to his namesake, producing credit after credit. He shoved them across the knotty board to the lodgekeeper. "Catherine," she said, giving her name though no one had asked for it.

I nodded, doing my best to ignore the tadpoles swimming behind my boozed-up eyes. The lodgekeeper reminded me of so many other women we'd encountered on our journeys around the globe. Nurses, policewomen, and the occasional traveling companion, each one appeared for fleeting moments, following another pattern. *"A rare_____ was spotted in the..." "There's a tournament in which one hundred of the very best TiMo Masters..."* Kash never gave these women anything for the information they provided.

No money, no companionship, nothing.

Yet strangers spilled their secrets like willing sacrifices strapping themselves to the altar and plunging the dagger through their hearts.

He sat on his perch, leaning across the bar top to whisper to this Catherine. "Heard you've had some Wem sightings 'round here."

She nodded, making triple chins from her usual double. "Sure 'ave," she said. "My husband caught sight of it while checkin' the traps along the tree line."

"Oh? And where's the mister now."

"Out," the woman answered. I drained my last pint and studied the spider's web pattern of beer foam left behind. Then, I slid off the stool, shoving it hard against the bar. Beer sloshed like gold ejaculate from Kash's bottle.

"Going to bed, buddy?" he asked.

Turning my full black eyes to Kash, I nodded in the affirmative.

I stumbled from the bar, weaving to the hallway where our room waited.

Once inside, my eyes adjusted to the black of the room, and again I caught sight of my reflection. "I'm a man," I whispered. "I am. I am a man."

Then, long, black, claw-like nails slammed into my field of vision, their owner tapping on the other side of the glass. The points struck against the window—the glass the only thing keeping me safe. Something approached from behind. I turned fast, ready to surprise whoever was sneaking up on me.

But I found no one.

Just Kash's orb floating at eye level. Not touching. Not yet.

But soon.

Ripples marred the sphere's silvered surface. Concentric circles of shiny liquid metal grew until they surpassed the surface area of the container. I stood trapped between the darkness and the doorway opening in the orb. With a sigh, I made my choice and entered. Shrieks, howls, garbled murmurings, trumpeting blasts, a cacophony of the TiMos as they came to greet their prodigal son's return. My mercury-tinted orb followed, like a loyal pet at the heels of its master.

***

Every bone ached inside my stretched skin. I awoke the next morning to Kash's empty, untouched bed beside my own. In the communal bathroom, the shower head sprayed like a vomiting toddler, sputtering heavy brown water onto my bare, golden skin. Pain shot through my body, from ankle to neck to knees, far more extensive than the dull aches of a simple hangover.

I dressed in jeans, covered a t-shirt with a red leather jacket borrowed from Kash. It made me look like some motorcycle tough.

A single orb followed me as I left the room.

I returned to the lobby and found my companion back at the makeshift bar. He'd changed, and wore nothing more than a pink, frilly bathrobe.

Catherine the Lodgekeeper's nightshirt hung down her body, but didn't extend far enough. My lips formed a tiny "O" of surprise that grew more pronounced with the appearance of another man, shirtless in flannel pajama pants, silver hair atop his head. He padded over on bare feet. First, he kissed Catherine.

Then, he embraced Kash and the two men locked lips.

I figured the stranger for Catherine's husband, the one she claimed had spotted Wem along the tree line. This man turned to me, eyes wide with unhinged delight on his face. For a moment, I blushed, believing the trio meant to proposition me to join whatever arrangement they'd conceived the night before.

"Piterachoo! *The* Piterachoo?" Like a sneeze, my old name passed the lips of the leering man.

I froze. I'd imagined this moment countless times before, both waking and dreaming. *"No, I'm Peter Chu."* A simple, direct correction. And yet...

I said nothing.

"That's not his name!" Even with his flesh sweaty and his breath reeking of rum, Kash's words were clear and direct. They brooked no room for opposition.

Once more the celebrated Kash Atkins had come to his partner's rescue.

The other man bowed, appearing chastised, yet, wearing a familiar condescending smirk all the same. "My apologies," he said. "I know you've changed so much since last we crossed paths."

Hearing the stranger speak confirmed my suspicions. I stumbled back, bumping against a barstool, knocking it to the ground. The resultant *clang* echoed through the otherwise empty lodge.

Kash whispered into my ear. "It's okay, Peter. It's okay."

Then, I realized the true identities of our lodgekeeper and her *husband*. "Billy and Kit," I said, spitting their names like a curse.

The duo, aged and altered in a way no less significant than what I'd undergone, responded in rehearsed unity, the way they'd done many times before. "The Tiny Monster Killers, at your service. Even if...you *don't* deserve us."

"It's not what you think, Peter," Kash said.

***

*Except it was.*

Billy and Kit, otherwise known as the Tiny Monster Killers, were now allied (and then some) with my former partner.

During our tournament days, the pair—brother and sister, lovers, *both?*—stalked us relentlessly. They left a trail of TiMo carcasses in their wake. As much fame and glory as Kash won, those two matched him in infamy and scorn.

The TMKs viewed TiMos as abominations. For all of their other eccentricities, the die-hard belief in the role of man as the sole inheritor of God's kingdom remained steadfast within them. I doubted their fundamentalism was so easily undone.

Pulled into a dark corner of the lodge, away from our former nemeses, I relayed all these concerns to Kash, reciting ancient history he already knew so well. The strain on my vocal cords no longer mattered, I wanted everything out in the light.

"Have things changed so much you'd use...*them?* You'll play their twisted games? Don't you remember what they do to TiMos? What they intend for my kind?"

Kash placed his hand, still smooth and soft the way I remembered, the hand of someone who asks another to fight but never does so himself, against my cheek. Again, he traced the scars I'd chosen for myself.

"But you're not one of *your* kind anymore, are you?"

I wanted to pull away and walk out the door, then find my own way back to the city. But I stayed.

After all, he had me dead to rights. The same way he'd captured me all those years before and put me in his orb—the first of his collection.

Back then, there was no one else inside his orb's pocket dimension. As a mucus-covered, embryonic fluid-sticky hatchling, I made for a pathetic quarry. Crying, alone, and abandoned, I floated in Kash's endless void, finding something close to peace.

I stayed there for an eternity, not even carrying an individual name but repeating that of my subspecies. *Piterachoo.*

"With their skills… Those two are the second-best at locating TiMos in the world. Behind you and me, of course."

I hated the way Kash included me, reminding me how much of the blame rested on my shoulders for what happened to my kind in our various forms, functions, and colors.

"Yow!"

He withdrew his hand. Pink flesh smoking, bearing the scent of cooked meat on a hot grill. Not even I could control myself when faced with this betrayal. Tears formed in his eyes to match my own.

"They're in my employ," he said, trying to talk through obvious pain. "We finalized the deal last night. That's why I didn't say anything earlier. You see, we need their help to track Wem. *Whatever it takes.*"

I stayed silent.

"One more, you understand? Wem's the last one I need. Then, I'll have captured them all."

"How's your collection these days?" I asked.

My question stopped him in his tracks, derailing whatever head of argumentative steam he'd prepared.

"They're fine," he said. "Like always."

*Lies.*

After all, I'd stood before the gathered council of my brothers and sisters the night before.

There was every variety of TiMo inside Kash Atkins's orb.

Except for two of us.

Wem—a rumor, a legend, a children's bedtime story brought to life through the sheer will of all those who dreamed to capture them. They possessed the power of darkness, the nothingness from which all life emerged. Those who whispered tales of Wem referred to them as "The Originator"—the source through which all other TiMos traced genetic lineage. Other, less reputable scholars even traced *humanity's* origins through Wem.

If true, then my purchased transformations came across not as hideous and blasphemous as I sometimes imagined in my darker, more melancholic moments.

The other TiMo missing from Kash's orb...was me.

That morning before the hunt, I contemplated whether I'd changed enough to retain my freedom? How far would my former lover, former friend, master, exploiter, and captor go to keep his collection whole?

What mattered more to him, catching us all...*or keeping us?*

I turned away, back to our old enemies at the bar. My eyes settled on the pelt of the TMKs' old TiMo traveling companion—a *Snff*—tacked onto the wall, a final trophy for the murderous twosome.

Their Snff helped hunt us for slaughter. He must've believed he'd escaped their wrath by doing so.

I watched Kash's Adam's apple rise and fall, as he observed the Snff's stretched skin. "I won't let them hurt you," he said.

Once more I wanted to believe him.

***

Kash's second-ever TiMo acquisition was a Tortalien. *Acquisition*: a word we've used to avoid saying *captive*. Kash's Tortalien, my old friend, still silver-skinned with black compact eyes like an insect and a brown turtle's shell on his back, stood on a raised dais made from several other TiMos.

"You help?" he asked, his voice sending tremors through me as I floated inside Kash's orb the evening prior.

Inside Kash's orb, I bore witness to bruised, puffy skin, scabs scratched open, and popped blisters oozing pus over fur, scale, and feathers alike. Even Cyborneans with their eighty-percent mechanical forms displayed rusted parts and frayed wires.

It was no longer a prized collection. I'd entered the TiMo equivalent of a puppy mill, where the whine of a wild-eyed, flame-breathing, tatter-winged Firemodo Dragwing set me on edge. Madness had spread like a rabies infection, passed back and forth in those isolated quarters.

"Let me help you" I demanded.

My words wouldn't reach all of them, I resorted to hand gestures, pantomiming.

"You. Monster. You. Man." Tortalien said.

With his black insectoid eyes regarding me from every angle, Tortalien's intentions still remained indecipherable. "What's it mean?" I asked.

"You here."

I nodded. *Yes, yes, of course.* I was there. Far from my adopted home. Far from any home I'd ever known. Before the egg broke, there was darkness. Then, I opened my eyes and power filled me beyond my minuscule frame.

"Where else would I go?" I asked.

They shook their heads. All of them. In unison.

"No. Always here."

I pulled out the scrap of paper.

"I know you sent this. I woke up and knew if I reached into my orb it'd be waiting for me. And it was."

When I looked at the paper again, the black ink bled across the white of the paper, smeared like a bug on a windshield.

***

Deep in the jungle, with Kash and the TMKs, a fire raged inside. Every step brought agony. But no one, not even the man who'd told me he loved me and lusted after me, looked back in response to my pained whining. Billy swung a laser machete with red-hot efficiency, slicing away jungle vines. Now and then, the yelps and death-rattles of unlucky TiMos in the path of his blade followed the downward swings.

Kit and Kash walked side-by-side, heads together, examining blips on equipment read-out screens. Tiny dark green blobs appeared across light green backgrounds. With everyone absorbed in the pursuit, we missed it as the noises of the lush rainforest slipped away like thieves in the night.

Darkness settled above a bird's nest. I said nothing and sounded no alarms.

Everything happened at once.

"There he is!" Kash shouted.

The human trio all had drool at the corners of their lips and their eyes were bloodshot.

Wem remained still. An unmoving, unflappable embodiment of night.

Kash reached for his orb. He spoke the traditional words preceding every TiMo match. "Orb, open give me—"

Before he finished, I shouted to the heavens, to the unseen stars. "Orb, open. Give me *everything*."

Kash whipped around, wild-eyed, spittle flying from his mouth. "But where's your or—oh!"

My orb—left inside Kash's the night before—blossomed. Infinite space inside infinite space creating an explosive paradox.

Shards of liquid metal flew through the air, ripping through Kit's face, sending her to the ground screaming.

And then, the colors.

So many colors, every single TiMo, fleeing from the confining orb.

When the smoke cleared, Kash was on his knees, moaning. A thin cut bled across his scalp.

Most of the TiMos were gone. But not all of them. Billy swung his blade like a battle-ax, cutting through winged TiMos, stabbing at crawling, creeping subspecies unlucky enough to cross his path. All the while, his sister-lover shouted her encouragement. "Kill them, Billy. Kill them! Kill 'em all."

When I looked into the trees, Wem sat perched, waiting.

I wanted to cry.

Before I made a sound, the TMKs tackled me to the ground, holding my arms, cinching tighter. I screamed. My whole body vibrated. An intense build-up of energy, both electrical and emotional, swirled inside my guts. Begging for release.

*I'd denied it for so long.*

The shock ripped through the murderous duo, searing flesh, charring it black until eyeballs popped, smoke leaking from emptied sockets. I wrenched myself free from their ashen embrace, leaving them fused into one black mass.

A fitting end.

I found Kash watching Wem. I don't know if he'd given the order to grab me or if they acted of their own murderous volition. I wasn't going to ask.

Wem extended an arm. First, he pointed to Kash. Then, to me.

Pink and gray brain matter dribbled down Kash's face. He wobbled like a tree rotted from the inside, waiting for a harsh storm to strike the final blow.

"Buddy?" The only thing he could say.

A flood of dark energy shot from the trees, thunderous in its approach.

I raised my hands, three fingers bent like claws, pinched to better direct the flow of the white-hot lightning as a counterstrike. I made my battle cry, calling my name so everyone knew who fought that day.

"Peter! Chu!"

I chose to fight again of my own free will. And whether for a final, fatal moment or for years to come, I'd live with that decision.

# THE DOGCATCHER

Not yet calling himself the Dogcatcher, he woke to find his naked body stretched across the limestone-slick entrance of a cliffside cavern overlooking a beach where the roaring ocean slapped at the rocks and sand. The salt spray from the incoming tide tickled his nose.

The Dogcatcher moaned. His eyes opened and he found himself the recipient of a tongue-bathing from head-to-toe as administered by a pack of scruffy, mangy mutts. One or two sniffed his ass and others licked his face over and over, insistent in their ministrations.

With a wet fart and an attempt at a roar which came out more like a hacking smoker's cough, the Dogcatcher lumbered to his feet. He moved too fast and had to steady himself with a hand on the matted fur of a dog. No smooth or silky coat there, touching the stiff hairs was like slamming his hand onto a bed of nails. Pulling his palm back with a surprised howl, he found the dog nonplussed at this unexpected and brief contact. After rocking back on the pink-skinned heels of his bare feet, the Dogcatcher leaned forward to gaze past the curving paunch of his belly. His prick poked past his stomach's curve, flaccid and wrinkled with the head resembling an ugly baby.

The Dogcatcher found his face and legs wet, sticky with drool, and seasoned by ocean winds. A scruffy-looking German Shepherd snuffled closer, aiming its wet, black snout in the direction of the Dogcatcher's crotch.

The man held a puffed-up, pale hand at snout level and shoved the dog away. The force used was harder than intended, but the distance achieved was not displeasing to the man.

In retreat, the Shepherd returned a high-pitched yelp, but soon regrouped, spinning on its back paws.

Jowls flared. A deep growl rumbled up from its throat. The Dogcatcher, sensing he'd gone too far, took a step back. The heel of his foot slid against the cavern entrance. The other dogs—the poodles, terriers, Dalmatians, Labradors, and more—followed the Shepherd's lead. Their choral growling reminded the Dogcatcher of the approach of a motorcycle gang, ripped jeans and patched-up leather vests, pulling into a dive bar parking lot.

For a moment, the Dogcatcher was grateful to extract a vivid sense-memory from the fog-shrouded corners of his addled mind. But when he remembered he didn't even know his name, dread and unease resumed their rightful place at the forefront of his mind.

A new dog barked, a sharp, stinging sound directed at the ears of the nude amnesiac. The Dogcatcher shuffled back again. When he turned his head and gazed into the endless dark of the cavern, a soul-gripping dread took hold, overwhelming the immediate fear of a bite from one of the pooches.

The assembled pack waited until the German Shepherd approved of the initial barker. When the old dog, with scars the Dogcatcher recognized as bullet wounds healed over in an infected, pus-yellow fashion, started in, the others joined. In doing so, they offered the Dogcatcher a closer look inside their maws. To his surprise, he found each dog's pink and black mottled gums devoid of teeth.

He tossed back his head and laughed. The orgiastic barking ceased. The old dogs placed paws over the sides of their heads. Rather than venturing deeper into the endless void of the unknown cavern, the Dogcatcher stepped forward, bold in his nakedness. Despite his apparent amnesia, he was assured in his superiority over the assembled mutts.

He shoved them out of the way with clubbing blows, knocking some back so close to the cliffside he soon heard the scratching and scraping of untrimmed tallow-colored nails against rock. When he got to the edge, the Dogcatcher peered down and his eyes widened.

The descending path, whether hewed into the cliff face by man or the elements, appeared navigable. But what waited below made the man gasp. *Another* pack of mangy, wild dogs, identical in breed make-up to the toothless, drooling, pathetic specimens on the cliff, waited with tongues wagging and almond-shaped eyes tilted in his direction. He noticed tiny teeth in their mouths and stained fur around their maws, a faded Kool-Aid red. The wind caught the right synchronized exhalation from the pups, sending the foul odor of decay up to the Dogcatcher's nose.

"Someone oughta take care of you dogs," the Dogcatcher said, speaking to himself more than the canines around him. Void of any solid memory from his past, he faced a serious decision: either fall into despair or embrace the bizarre challenges laid before him.

It surprised him when the dogs on the beach parted, revealing an ironed and pressed grey woolen uniform waiting atop a towel over the sand. The Dogcatcher considered his naked body and how a cold, salty breeze made his balls shrivel. Then, he considered the clothes waiting for him.

They looked close enough to his size.

Watching his steps, casting glances back and forth between the two packs, the Dogcatcher crept to the sandy beach under the cliffside. When he stepped off the path, he brought his hands together, clapping loud and making shouting sounds to match, driving the dogs away. "Go on! Get back! Get!"

The dogs obeyed.

The Dogcatcher inspected the gray uniform shirt—short-sleeved and well-starched. The standard-issue tightie-whiteys, grey slacks cinched with a black belt, plus black socks, and black shoes. Those shiny black shoes could've caught the Dogcatcher's reflection if he leaned his bulk forward more.

The uniform did fit. From socks and shoes to underwear and pants. Even the crew-neck white t-shirt hugged his frame. When it came time to don his short-sleeved grey uniform shirt, the no-longer-naked man turned the shirt over to consider its front.

Someone had sewn a cloth nametag above the left shirt pocket. The Dogcatcher brought the shirt closer, hoping the clothes belonged to him and offered some clue to his identity. He hoped they'd trigger a flood of memories, returning him to a world of sense.

One wish came true. The uniform *was* his. In the oval sewn above the pocket, he read the word "DOGCATCHER." Perhaps he'd wanted something more? To be called a Gary or Steve or Steven, Claude, Daryl, Nebuchadnezzar?

A title was better than nothing. The Dogcatcher sighed and pulled his arms through the sleeves. His fingers fumbled with the flat, pearl-white buttons threading them through the thin slits of the buttonholes. Soon enough, he'd finished.

Rocking back on his heels, feeling the heat of the woolen uniform as clouds parted and the sun emerged, the Dogcatcher wiped the back of his hand across his already sweating brow and asked "Well, now what?"

The yelp of a sleeker, younger dog—younger even than the pack assembled on the beach—served as answer. The other dogs parted and a grey-furred hound, about the same color gray as the Dogcatcher's uniform, emerged. The dog was barely past puppyhood, still energetic and powerful but somewhat restrained and reserved in its nature.

The dog took bounding steps to cover the distance between it and the Dogcatcher. Moving fast enough to catch the man by surprise, its rapid approach sent him stumbling backward. The hound leaped, placing its paws on the Dogcatcher's shoulders. A tongue like a roll of pink deli meat flopped from its jowls. The Dogcatcher recoiled at the touch of the wet, steamy tongue on his cheeks, the musk from the dog's breath overwhelming his nostrils.

The Dogcatcher grabbed the green braided collar around the mutt's neck. Once he held it, he shoved the creature away. "Get off me, dammit!"

For whatever trouble he'd caused, the new dog appeared concerned enough with being a *good boy* to modify his behavior. He sat on lean haunches, tail patting the sand and sending up tiny clouds with every impact.

The Dogcatcher caught sight of a folded piece of paper secured between the collar and the dog's neck. With cautious fingers, he snatched the note away, pulling it close.

*Follow me to the City.* When he finished reading, the Dogcatcher supplied his own commentary. "Well, *that* doesn't tell me much."

The hound must've sensed—or even understood—that the note was read and its message conveyed to the Dogcatcher. Its tail still wagging, the dog made a brisk run up the beach, heading toward dunes and a set of weather-worn wooden steps. It turned its head at one point, not stopping but slowing enough to make sure the Dogcatcher followed.

Hoping for answers and contact with other humans, the Dogcatcher trailed behind the hound as they crossed the sands. Coarse gray and white pulverized rocks poured over the top of and into his black plastic-coated uniform shoes with every step toward the walkway. When he reached the exit, he was red-faced and winded.

The Dogcatcher leaned against the stair railing, catching his breath. He looked back the way he'd come. The cave dogs were gone, having abandoned their cliffside gathering. He wondered if they'd ventured into the expansive darkness of the cavern. Meanwhile, the beach dogs ascended the now unoccupied cliff. The Dogcatcher tilted his head, believing he'd picked out a tinkling, akin to falling shards of broken glass, carried back to him on the virulent wind. The sun hung heavy over the clear blue sky illuminating the coastal scene. *Were those teeth falling on the rocks from the bleeding mouths of the curs?*

Free from the sand, the Dogcatcher's speed increased by several degrees. The rhythmic clap of his thick-heeled shoes against the aged wood announced his presence to whomever or whatever waited beyond the crest of the dunes.

When he reached the top, the Dogcatcher bent over, wheezing from the slight exertion of removing his shoes and watching the sand pour from them like he'd smashed an hourglass open. When he straightened from this last task, he took in the *City* beyond the beach

The Dogcatcher crossed to a boardwalk where sunglass kiosks mingled with soda shops serviced by roller-skating wait staff and everyone's skin was perfect. The people waved and smiled at each other. Once they caught sight of the Dogcatcher, every person waved and smiled at him.

But they'd stop short, wrinkling their noses—the way one might respond to the sight of some mustache-twirling villain galivanting about town after tying the helpless damsel to the railroad tracks. If the Dogcatcher noticed this chilly reception, he gave no indication. In truth, the sudden presence of other human beings and the accompanying signs of garish civilization all around them served as enough of a distraction.

He placed a hand over his brow, shielding himself from the explosion of cream-colored buildings and people, all bordered with bright colors like sugar cookie frosting. But when his initial scan proved fruitless, the uniformed man reached for one of the passing citizens.

"Excuse me, madam," he said to an old woman with a back crooked into a near question-mark while she moved beneath the shade of the floppy white canvas sun hat covering her silver hair, "Have you by chance seen a dog? A hound I mean. With grey fur. And a green collar?"

The old woman met the eyes of the Dogcatcher and the sour purse of her features in response to his presence was unmistakable. He swallowed, licking his teeth with a tongue leaden and unwieldy inside his mouth, as he wondered whether his breath had made the woman recoil so. But her attention fell to his uniform. More specifically, on the *word* sewn above the pocket. It took the Dogcatcher a moment to catch on.

*Dogcatcher.*

Realizing how the label came across, especially given his earlier query, the man sighed and put on a cheerful expression he hoped better matched the Americana ambience he'd stumbled upon. "Oh. No. I'm not looking for it because of *this*."

He struck a finger across the *Dogcatcher* patch, providing a symbolic denial of his role. However, he'd no other name to offer the woman.

She woman nodded. Her features showed no signs of softening.

"The dog, madam?" he prompted.

She remained silent but extended her arm, pointing the way forward, deeper into the City. The Dogcatcher tilted his head like the hound back on the beach. A curious notion struck the man.

The Dogcatcher wasn't certain he'd witnessed any of the citizens he'd encountered uttering a single word. But how to dig deeper? *"Pardon me, madam, please say something. Anything?"* Instead, the Dogcatcher opted to tip an imaginary hat and head in the direction the elderly woman indicated.

The wooden boardwalk gave way to concrete sidewalks and black asphalt-paved roads. Based on the long shadows across the buildings and the muggy weather blanketing the urban landscape in a musky haze, the Dogcatcher figured the time of year for the dog days of summer.

The Dogcatcher sought the cooler side of every sidewalk he wandered along. He stopped under every available awning. He still hoped to catch sight of the dog who'd brought him into town. Once or twice, he observed a wagging tail or wrinkled his nose having smelled some tree doused in dog piss.

But there was no direct contact with the dog he sought. As his plan to find the pooch evaporated, he formulated new strategies for curing his amnesia. For all the kitschy shops and restaurants glimpsed along the way, the Dogcatcher found no trace of anything resembling a government or any form of authority.

No police station, no firehouse, not even signs outlining speed limits or reminding citizens not to litter, jaywalk, et cetera, et cetera. Whenever the Dogcatcher moved to stop a passing citizen, they swerved out of his way.

When two children, a boy with a lollipop as big as the bottom half of his face and a girl walking a white, silky-furred kitten on a pink leather leash, skipped past the Dogcatcher before the man finished a

"Hello," something snapped inside the lost soul. He lunged forward, not expecting to catch anything. But soon, the young boy's bare skin gave way against his fingertips.

The boy's mouth fell open as if to scream, cry, or curse the Dogcatcher. Indeed, twin fat tear dollops gathered in the corners of his eyes. The girl glared at the Dogcatcher, her look conveying so much more than words. "Look, tell me..." The Dogcatcher stopped short of making a full demand though.

A dog barked and the Dogcatcher aborted his efforts to communicate with the boy and girl. He let go of the boy's arm and shooed the pair away. As though to say, *run along now children, the adults are going to talk.* The children seemed more than happy to follow his unspoken order.

A German Shepherd pup bounded over, stopping inches from the Dogcatcher.

A crackling, static-filled voice emanated from the dog's collar, as the voice addressed the confused man. "Dogcatcher, you're back."

The Dogcatcher took a knee, bringing him to eye level with the pup. But he addressed the voice emanating from the collar. "Who're you?" he asked.

"I'm the Police Dog."

The Dogcatcher extended his hand toward the mutt whose eyes gleamed yellow and whose muscular future-form remained visible beneath its puppy-soft, rounded body. But as the mini-beast's black lips curled back revealing teeth growing long, white, and healthy inside pink gums, the Dogcatcher stopped short. He drew his shaking hand back and wiped it across his brow.

"I...I understand what...*it* is," he said, gesturing at the dog. "But what...who *are* you?"

"I'm the Police Dog. I'm the Police Dog. I'm the Police Dog."

That was enough. The Dogcatcher stood, causing his shadow to fall across the pup.

"I'm the Police Dog."

The Dogcatcher waved a dismissive hand at the pup. "Yeah, okay. Whatever, pal."

He took his first step past the Shepherd. Then another. And another. But with a sudden growl, the dog sprinted and blocked the Dogcatcher's exit. The man's brow wrinkled in frustration. He shouted to the other people moving along the periphery of the strange scene in which he'd found himself. "Hey! Hey! Anybody know what's going on with this dog? Who's it belong to?"

No one answered. No one hung their heads or even turned away to pretend like the Dogcatcher wasn't there. They went on with their lives, pantomiming the day-to-day existence of a small seaside town bustling with seaside town activity. They moved as child's playthings made to bop to the rhythm of nursery rhyme tunes.

Still, the Dogcatcher persisted. "Whose dog is this?"

Again, nothing.

Except for the voice still emanating from the collar. "I'm the Police Dog."

"Fine. You're the Police Dog. And I'm…"

The German Shepherd barked. The Dogcatcher's stomach—empty and overheated, billowing with gas and sick—responded with sudden intensity to the canine yelp. The voice spoke again. "You're the Dogcatcher. And once again, you've violated our treaty. I'm afraid I need to take you into the Tower for your punishment."

"Tower? Treaty? Punishment? Look, Mr. 'Police Dog,' I don't know what the hell you're talking about."

In waiting for a chance to flee, the Dogcatcher noticed something familiar in the coloration of the Police Dog. Not the generic black-and-tan of *any* German Shepherd, but a near identical color pattern to the older dog he'd met on the cliffside. The Dogcatcher wondered if the old dying dog was any relation.

*It stood to reason in a town so small.*

And yet, with each passing moment, the Dogcatcher understood Dog City as far from any definition of *reasonable*. His eyes darted, impatience growing. He had a junkie's urge for movement, even if it meant destruction (self or otherwise). "Look, Police Dog, all I want is to figure out who the hell I am and how to get the hell out of here. But back that way's the ocean," he said, hitching his thumb behind him to indicate the path he'd already traveled. "So, if you wanna escort me to the other side of town, I'll mosey on out of your weird city limits and get help from actual human beings."

The goddamn dog shook its head. "Come with me to the Tower to face your punishment."

The Dogcatcher sighed. A tremor traveled through his body. His fast-beating heart banged against the prison bars of his rib cage. He blew out a long breath. Sour stomach acid reflux burned his throat. He cleared it away with a swallowed growl of his own, then answered. "Okay, okay. Give me a minute to tie my shoe."

He bent to the ground, fingers working the laces. Whistling while he worked. Then, he popped up with one of his cheap black plastic shoes in hand.

"Fuck this!" He paired the exclamation with a hard throw, launching the shoe so its heel smashed against the snout of the pup, eliciting a sharp yelp.

Every person in the vicinity ceased their activity. They moved like automatons, heading toward the whining Police Dog. The creature's eyes watered like they could cry real tears. Like a person.

The Dogcatcher refused to wait for the drama to follow. Instead, he took off at a full sprint, or at least as close to one, as his bulk and the uneven nature of his gait (minus one shoe) allowed. He didn't stop to ask for help. He ignored any person, young, old, man, or woman he came across. And he kept his eyes low to the ground. Hiding in alleys between city blocks and catching his breath when possible, he strained to separate his wheezing from the "heh-heh-heh" rhythmic panting of more dogs on his heels.

Shop and apartment lobby doors slammed open. More and more of Dog City's human residents took to the streets. The sharp crack of reinforced steel-framed doors against brick building facades sounded like the distant collective baying of a pack of hounds when it reached the Dogcatcher's ears.

His head on a swivel, searching for a place to hide, his skin itched, as the sweat-soaked woolen clothes chafed his sunburn. Growing more desperate and confused by the moment, thanks to his every effort at communication fizzling like dud firecrackers on a rainy day, he sought respite from the silent people who stalked him through the streets, each one acting in obeisance to the Police Dog whom he believed was given their collective voice. The Dogcatcher choked back a relieved sob when he spotted a construction site a few feet ahead. It appeared abandoned, a tattered condominium company pasteboard sign shredded by past high winds giving evidence of a project forsaken.

The Dogcatcher picked up a salt and fish odor as he walked across the compact red clay dirt on the ground, as though the ocean he'd run from had moved much farther inland. With more time and a level head, he'd wonder how the ocean musk reached that spot, yet remained otherwise imperceptible along and through the streets he'd already passed. However, not wishing to ask more questions, the desperate man raced between steel girders laying out the building's skeleton.

His arms pumping to match the snare drum beat of his heart, the Dogcatcher lost control and one clenched fist slammed against the hot metal of a solid silver beam. The impact caused the blanched white skin stretched across his knuckles to split, peeling it back like a reopened wound scratched by an ambitious toddler. The blow's echo resounded, as though the whole building's skeleton rattled.

The Dogcatcher spun around. He found no one and no dogs behind him. He raised the bleeding knuckle to his chapped and swollen lips. A taste of hot pennies coated his tongue as he sucked blood oozing from the split skin. The hand ached. His ears rang.

*Woof!*

The gruff bark sent shivers down the Dogcatcher's spine. He checked again, back where he'd come from. Then, he looked ahead, peering through the crisscross pattern of steel beams and shadows.

*Woof!*

Again, he checked in front and behind, anticipating the sight of some dog or a whole pack of the four-legged beasts bounding toward him.

*Woof!*

A heavy snorting and panting reached the Dogcatcher's ears. He cursed under his breath, frustrated by the way fear gripped him and by his inability to perform the task for which he wore the uniform. After all, if he was the Dogcatcher, then shouldn't it be much easier for him to...catch a dog?

Something wet struck the man's brow, then trickled into his open eye before he blinked. The antiseptic liquid burned on contact. His bloody hand slapped near his forehead, wiping at whatever liquid had fallen against his sunburnt skin. Something wet and foamy mingled with the leaking serum from his self-inflicted wound. Once free from the expectorant, the Dogcatcher looked up to the place where his eyes met those of a bulldog with a body like a lump of uncooked dinner-roll dough.

Despite its size and shape, the bulldog balanced on the beam above the Dogcatcher's head with no issue.

"Hey, Police Dog, Construction Dog here. I found the naughty, naughty Dogcatcher. He's at my building site, sneaking and sneaking."

"The fuc—"

Before the Dogcatcher finished his epithet, the bulldog threw its whole body, rolls and all, off the structural-beam perch. It made a rapid descent with jowls flopping as gravity finished the job. The Dogcatcher found his arms filled with the flour-sack-heavy body of the mutt.

Four stubby paws scrambled for purchase, tearing at the Dogcatcher's uniform and striking his sunburnt skin in equal measure. "You're not allowed on this building site without a permit, Dogcatcher." The lifeless intonations came from the bulldog's collar, even as its teeth sunk into the man's slick, sweat-soaked flesh.

In a desperate bid for relief, he squeezed meaty handfuls of dog flesh in both hands. Seizing the wrinkled pooch, he tore it loose. Flesh and cloth came away. "Get off of me!"

He threw the squirming dog hard against a steel beam. The crack of its skull and the thud of its twitching, soon-to-be-dead body against the ground followed.

"Damn dog," the Dogcatcher muttered.

He launched himself deeper into the skeletal remains of the construction site. His spiking adrenaline kept him upright. Even as every part of him ached through his sodden clothing, the Dogcatcher knew stopping to recover wasn't an option.

The building site took up several city blocks. Rich, cake-like dirt sprayed to knee level on the Dogcatcher's uniform, as the German Shepherd ambushed him. A poodle growled from across the street, resting on a window ledge.

The Dogcatcher stomped his foot in the muddy ground. The black sole of his work boot dragged a divot through the earth. Still, he held up his hands, sensing he'd run out of second chances.

"Alright," he said, "take me to your Tower."

"First, pick up Construction Dog and bring him with you," the Police Dog or the person speaking through the Police Dog—*though the Dogcatcher wasn't even certain there was much difference*—commanded.

The Dogcatcher obeyed, scooping the ruined, wrinkled body of the bulldog into his arms. He held its corpse against his chest. With an escort on land and one covering the rooftops above and the jangle of an ID tag on the dead bulldog filling the silences between every step taken, the Dogcatcher completed his journey to the Tower.

The structure was unlike anything he'd ever seen before. Something old—ancient even—in its outer shell. Old stones carved from lost, forsaken mountains.

His arms ached. Having no desire to face either the black and brown eyes of the Police Dog or the poodle he'd dubbed *Flying Dog* because of her elegant leap from her raised perch, the Dogcatcher balked at waiting for confirmation from the canines on what should happen next. Instead, he went ahead and bent down, placing the Construction Dog's limp form at the base of the tower, making an offering. Where he'd placed the cold, heavy corpse, a section of the wall slid away. Moments later, an army of puppies padded out, taking up their places around their fallen brethren.

The Dogcatcher kept his distance from the mourners. He watched, as one by one, each pup licked the dead bulldog.

Teeth rubbed against the skin of the hand hanging by the Dogcatcher's side. The German Shepherd pup took a couple of the man's fingers in its maw. The tiny creature padded forward, pulling on the skin, bringing the man with it. Its teeth didn't sink in deep enough to break flesh or draw blood.

But they went deep enough so the Dogcatcher got the message. He followed the pup, moving past the throng of furry whelps and their dead comrade laying in the center of their grieving circle. Before he reached the opening from which the pups emerged, the Dogcatcher looked straight up to the top of the tower. He spied a symbol, something like a dog's paw but twisted in on itself and set sideways. It reminded the Dogcatcher of an infinity symbol. A chuckle like a dying man's tubercular cough escaped his lips.

It amused him to not know his name but to recall the concept of the infinite.

"You're the Dogcatcher," the Police Dog answered as though it'd read the man's thoughts.

"Oh, what do you know?" the Dogcatcher answered, giving himself over to the absurdity of his situation.

The stone slid behind the Dogcatcher and he found himself alone in darkness. Alone with a pack of dogs. Some panted. Others growled. The heavy perfume of the canid breath proved a blend of sweat and shit.

Loose fur drifted past, as though a slight breeze penetrated through some unseen crack in the not-so-perfect stone façade.

Voices from the darkness reached the Dogcatcher's ears. "Dogcatcher, you've returned from exile in blatant violation of the sentence delivered by the Council of Whelps."

Even though he trembled with fear, the Dogcatcher found his voice inside the black, musty space where the dogs had corralled him. "I don't know what you're talking about. I woke on the beach with no memory. No name. Except for what came written on my clothes here."

A cacophony of barking accompanied glimpses of sharp white teeth too close to the bare flesh of his hands. The Dogcatcher pulled those hands close to his chest. The voice of the dog or whoever spoke for the dogs continued reading out his crimes. "In addition, you're accused of the murder of the Construction Dog: our loyal friend and a diligent servant to the metropolis of Dog City. Construction Dog built our home from the dirt, fulfilling our destiny."

The Dogcatcher held his tongue, not wanting to risk incurring the wrath of the dogs in the dark. But then, as though someone read his mind once more, fluorescent light flooded the cavernous chamber. Electric sconces set in columns winding up the stone faces. Witnessing the sheer number of pups surrounding him was intimidating enough for the Dogcatcher, even after he'd already gotten a sense of their grand cohort while bathed in the darkness.

They spoke in a million voices echoing off the tower walls. "We find you guilty."

The Dogcatcher shook his head. The musk and heat made his clothes stick to his skin, holding him tight all over like a spider's web ensnaring some tasty morsel. A new madness overtook the man. As he worked the buttons of his shirt, peeling off shoes and socks next, the Dogcatcher experienced a sense of profound relief, unburdening himself of those itchy articles of clothing.

He stood naked before the assembled pack. He let moisture withdraw from his every pore. Even with puddles of sweat falling from his nude form to cover the cement floor at his feet, the Dogcatcher remained an island amid the sea of canines.

They kept their distance. Indeed, they even moved into the *sit* position. Tails whisking the ground, sending up clouds of dust. The Dogcatcher grinned. Every single dog sat before him.

His red, sweaty hand snaked down his front and he pulled on his flaccid chubby little cock. The smooth pink head and the spotted gray on his soft shaft. *I'm a man. These dogs are my best friends. They're nothing more than dumb, dumb animals.*

"Sit!"

His voice sounded so much smaller than the earlier choral yapping of the pack.

Still, they remained seated.

"Stay!"

The Dogcatcher, who remained the Dogcatcher even though he'd taken off the uniform and denied the title, stepped forward. His body sought an opening between a mangy hound and a Labrador retriever who looked as if it'd come from a swim at the beach. He'd use the gap to facilitate his escape. Or so he hoped.

The rhythmic panting of the pups filled his ears.

*Heh. Heh. Heh. Heh.*

*Heh. Heh. Heh. Heh.*

Once he'd made it outside the circle of canines, the Dogcatcher searched high and low for some egress from the tower. "Stay," he repeated.

His search came up short. He found no stairs leading up, nor any visible trigger meant to open the surrounding wall encircling him and the dogs.

"Down!"

This time, the *dogs* gave the order. As the cement floor slid out from under his feet, the naked, confused Dogcatcher's uncovered ass hit the curved embrace of a long silver slide, a curving monstrosity that appeared to plunge into the earth, down to Hell itself. With the slide stored in a tight, compact manner under the floor, its metal surface gave off an intense heat. It burnt the Dogcatcher's rear, causing his flesh to bubble and blister. Eruptions of blood, so red it'd turned a shade of violet, followed

The Dogcatcher scrambled for purchase, stretching his hands to the side to find something to get a grip on and slow his descent. But he grabbed the sharp edges of the slide, the metal untreated and left ragged. The rusting metal ripped through the skin and meat of his fingers.

The Dogcatcher screamed. His voice turned to a choked, blubbery sob. Even with his momentum increased, the flesh torn from his body, and his fingers severed at the joints by the razor-edged border of the slide, he also picked out the sounds of too many puppies, bringing up the rear. Howling, barking, and yapping behind him.

The pups of Dog City chased the Dogcatcher, upsetting the natural balance as far as the man understood it. He should chase *them*, not the other way around. He contemplated dogs building cities, enforcing laws, flying, and more. The curs and bitches wanted so bad to become human, and yet they couldn't even play their parts as dogs well. They came tumbling down the slide, their poise perfected from frequent use. They nipped at the bloody, roasted chunks sloughing off the naked Dogcatcher's injured form.

They consumed his flesh. Intense pain shot through what remained of his body, until his trip down the slide came to a sudden and definitive end.

The Dogcatcher fell, crashing to a cavern floor, where rigid, gnarled stalagmites stabbed through his neck and pierced his genitals and taint.

As his consciousness faded, the dying man made a final effort to lift his head. Like how a naughty dog props his forepaws on a counter, seeking unattended morsels. He took in the strange sight of a room built into the cave. With this sight came the realization he'd reached the same cave from the beach, even though this conclusion made no sense. Inside the room, images of someone who looked like the Dogcatcher flickered with strobe-light intensity. The faces all looked like his face, but *wrong*. Like something else peered from under the surface, something with different eyes. If he paused for a  moment and went frame-by-frame, the Dogcatcher could call out these discrepancies and more. He'd apply a name to each of the incarnations. *Dogcatcher 2, Dogcatcher 3, and so on.*

Then, he heard a voice. *His* voice droning on inside the no-longer-hidden room: "You're not a dog. You're a man. You're not a dog, you're a man..."

The pups landed on his back in a never-ending pile of fur and meaty paws with claws out, teeth sharp and biting. The mass of furry flesh drove the rocky outcroppings deeper into the Dogcatcher's skin. Then, teeth sank into loosened flesh. The pups growled like they'd found their favorite chew toy all at once and none of them wished to relinquish their claim.

They pulled and pulled and pulled...

***

The bitch and her litter spilled from the Dogcatcher skin suit. The engorged teats of the dying mother offered some final sustenance to her mewling pink whelps until they opened their eyes and ascended, taking on the roles of Police Dog, Construction Dog, Flying Dog, Fire Dog, and more.

The latest Fire Dog gripped the rubber hose of the flamethrower in his mouth. He squeezed the trigger between his jaws until a thin line of gas oxygenated and a bloom of fire spread across the remains of the latest Dogcatcher skin suit.

The next bitch, her womb filled with the next generation of Dog City lay still while the most recent puppies pulled the new skin, another set pulled from the rack, over her form. She'd already changed. She thought like a human. She experienced the world as a human. In all its ugly and confusing details. Water ran down her eyes staring out at her former fellow dogs through the eyeholes of the Dogcatcher skin.

*Tears.* They called them tears.

She stood on her back paws. Experiencing new pressure from her awkward, undog-like stance. But she wasn't a dog anymore. She'd become the Dogcatcher. She'd get plenty of time to adjust to standing in the proper fashion. To move and talk like him. Then, her fellow aging pups would lead her to the beach. When they finished, they'd put her down and raise their next Dogcatcher.

She wondered what other animals filled the human skin suits of Dog City. She wondered if any of them even called their home "Dog City." Like the postman made of squirrels? Or the librarian filled with cats?

Someone told her humans were once filled with themselves. But this bitch found that hard to believe.

# The Secret Society of Schrödinger's Children

For as long as they were lost, the Children wore masks and were neither alive nor dead. But once someone found one of the Children as they were in the *real* world, then that boy or girl was definitively alive. Or definitively dead. They'd leave their mask for the next new child initiated into the Society.

The membership requirements were simple enough to join, but specific nonetheless:

(1) you have to join as a child and (2) the world out there can't know if you're alive or dead.

Sometimes, "the world out there" meant parents. However, for plenty of Children in the Society, existence depended upon their final fates remaining a mystery to caseworkers or police detectives or a social studies teacher who stared through the blinds of her classroom while a cloud of chalk dust falls on her robin's egg blue cardigan, wondering what happened to the girl in the back of the class who always wore long sleeves no matter the weather.

In the case of this particular member of the Society, her name was Grace, a sight easier to remember than "the girl in the back of the class who always wore long sleeves no matter the weather."

Grace came to the Society like all of its other members. One minute she was not a member of the organization, then she was. She materialized in the cafeteria line wearing a sundress showing her thin, bared arms and legs, pale skin mottled with greens and purples, deep royal blues. The other Children, marking her arrival, whispered about the new girl with a body colored in the manner of the Earth when viewed from outer space. All their quiet words reached Grace because no secrets exist among the Society's Children. She smiled under her new mask.

After she'd filled up in the cafeteria line, Grace sat down with a plate of macaroni and cheese, cooked carrots, chocolate pudding, and soda pop. She held up her spoon and studied the mask given by the Society. In the contorted reflection, she witnessed a black-eyed, black-beaked blue-feathered bird's head studying her right back.

Then, Grace touched a pale unblemished hand—smaller than those of the other girls in her old classes from her old life—to the feathered mask, confirming the new avian visage as hers.

"What do you figure, new girl, you alive or dead?"

The speaker, whose voice sounded soft at first but ended with a rattle like a poisonous snake, wore a skull mask, bone-white detailing outlined in black. They sat close by Grace, their hands stopping short of touching the new girl's mask. Grace stared into the coal-black pits of the skull mask's eye-sockets. The skull-mask wearer dropped their hand lower, holding it out the way an adult does when play-acting formality with a child. Shaking their hand, looking them in the eye.

Grace's arms hung by her sides though. Old fears flared up—her body dry kindling and this stranger's question a long match struck true. "Um, excuse me?"

"Are you alive? Or are you dead?" Her inquisitor repeated their line of questioning.

Grace studied the still-extended hand, finding something stiff and angular in its placement the longer it went unaccepted. The nail beds of the offered hand were black, and the stink of soil and night-crawlers wafted from the offered appendage. Grace considered how the skull-mask wearer appeared a head or two shorter than her. She wondered how old her inquisitor was.

"I'm here," she said, "Doesn't that mean I'm alive?"

The rattling voice emerging from the skull-mask-covered face became a hissing, gasping laugh. A high-pitched whistling so sharp and intense, Grace had to cover her ears. Or at least the feathered portion of the mask set over her ears.

Then, another hand touched her shoulder. She spun around in her seat, pulling away from this new presence. "Don't mind, Grim," the new Child—who wore an old t-shirt and ripped blue jeans with a droopy basset hound face mask covering their features, except for spikes of bleached blonde hair poking out from the dog's ears and jowls—said.

This new voice reminded Grace of sunshine, toes wiggling in wet beach sand after a wave rolls in and teases the shoreline. Comforted, she took the dog-faced boy's offered hand. "My name's Marvin," he said. "Welcome to the Society!"

From behind them, a gravelly "I'm sorry if I came on strong there," followed.

Grace, living up to her name, turned and shook the skull-masked Child's hand, which felt cold and clammy, with bathtub wrinkles on each digit. "Is your name *really* Grim?" Grace asked them once their handshake ended.

"Is your name really Grace?"

Before the new girl puzzled out the question, Marvin interrupted. "Grim believes they're special enough for a code-name. Like we're heroes or something."

"We could be," Grim mumbled, swiping a handful of carrots from Grace's plate.

Grace didn't mind. She sat still, letting Marvin (and Grim to a lesser extent) fill her in on the requirements for both joining and leaving the Society. She learned about the masks, though what her companions shared amounted to more or less what she'd already assumed. When they finished, Grace's questions still bubbled up inside. Her blood pumped under her motley-colored skin as a proxy.

"But what do we *do*?" she asked. Marvin and Grim exchanged inscrutable looks across Grace.

***

The trio, Grace and her unofficial welcoming committee, waited behind the bushes of the hospital. A children's hospital, but not a Children's hospital. Grace tripped over an uneven cement chunk of sidewalk. Both Marvin and Grim took one of her hands to steady her.

Adults and other children walked past the trio, giving them not even a glance back. It wasn't Halloween, yet the three Children of indeterminate age wore masks. And not some cheap department store masks either.

Marvin let go of Grace's hand once he was sure she'd recovered. When he did, he leaned close and whispered, "Look at the hairs on the backs of the children's necks."

Grace watched a thin boy in a bathrobe, tubes emerging from his body connected to a pole with sacks of fluid attached. The oversized covering, draped over the boy's form, drooped at his neck. With a little concentration, Grace saw the world anew, through the bird's eyes of her mask.

Hairs stood stiff on the boy's back. As if his physical form knew them, but his mind refused to process their breach of reality.

A cough from Grim pulled the new girl's attention away from the dying child and his entourage. "Don't worry about him," the skull-masked kid said, "Every single goddamn person in his life'll know when *he's* dead. No mistaking it. No need for him to wear a mask."

The sliding doors to the hospital's entrance opened before the three members of the Society. Then, they closed. Opened and closed. The masked trio held hands forming a line in front of the entryway. Passersby going in and out of the hospital swerved around the trio without a word, as though avoiding an ill-placed puddle.

Grace never liked silences in her old life. "Are we going in?" she asked.

"Maybe, maybe not," Grim answered.

"Grim!" Though impossible to read expressions under the face-covering masks they wore, and only loosened at the jawline during mealtimes, Grace was certain she *heard* the scowl in Marvin's reprimand.

Marvin turned his hound dog droopy-cheeked visage to her and said, "He means, the Director sent us here, but they never tell us *why* they're sending us somewhere. We're supposed to...figure it out, I guess. So, we wait...until we're sure about what we're supposed to do."

Grace nodded. "I understand," she said. Except she didn't understand.

She held back a bevy of questions ready to burst through the seams of her mask. "Who's this Director? When will I meet them? Are they a member of our Society? Or something else? Are they in charge?"

The last question chewed up the girl's insides. Having someone in charge was supposed to mean something. There had to be someone to make the rules, to set the examples. To lead the way and keep her safe.

"Heh."

"Grace?" Marvin's voice contained a tiny uptick of concern.

"Heh. Heh. Heh. Heh." The bird-masked girl's laughter came in fits and starts until it exploded out of her. Her true face moved under the mask, her lips turning up into a grin that grew as more chuckles escaped.

She doubled over, hands clutching her sides. Marvin kept his distance, but held his hands in front of his chest, like the dog whose face he wore, begging for treats. "Are you...should I...?"

Unlike his comrade, Grim embraced the sudden bout of mirth and joined in, laughing alongside the new girl. His laughter sounded like wet leaves against headstones. When he caught his breath, Grim said, "I take back what I told you earlier, Marvin. I like ol' Bird-Brain here."

Grace cut short her chuckles, snapping to attention. "Wait. You didn't like me?"

Grim shrugged. "To be fair, I don't like most Children. But it's all I get at the Society. So, c'est la vie, et cetera."

The girl shrugged right back. *Fair enough.* Then, she added, "But don't even think about sticking me with *Bird-Brain.*"

"Yeah, yeah, back to the drawin—"

"Grim, shut up."

Marvin slapped the flat of his palm against the other's shoulder. Through the hollow echo of his mask, his voice came loud like a cur's bark and sharp as a bite. Both the other Children turned to face the hospital's entrance.

Through the glass, they watched people meandering through the lobby, either heading for the exit or checking in with the security guard at the tall black reception desk a few feet from the entry point. Others wandered to the first-floor reception area or the elevator banks leading to the upper floors. The floors with sick children. Dying children. Nothing out of the ordinary for a children's hospital though. Nothing to remark upon, nothing except for the day-to-day triumphs and tragedies of those who deal in matters of sickness or health, life or death.

But then, Grace and Grim looked closer and noticed the woman, with her hair pulled back tight and an oversized pink hoodie draped over the upper part of her body. A large piece of clothing, its hem fell just above her knees. She'd zipped it to her neck. The pink body-covering sweatshirt and the woman's pale, sweaty face reminded Grace of an earthworm, wriggling up to the surface after a thunderstorm soaked the soil between the cracks in a sidewalk.

The woman's wide-eyed expression betrayed a turmoil barely contained beneath the surface. She held her eyes open, unblinking until a thin line of tears trickled down her cheeks and her lip quivered. Not to the point where anyone asked her what was wrong, but enough so they'd give her space. Let her figure things out for herself.

She looked innocent. Lost and innocent.

"Yeah, so wha—"

When Marvin moved to slap his palm against Grim a second time, the other Child intercepted the dog-mask boy's hand. Grim shook their head. It reminded Grace of the boys in her health class who'd played with the life-size skeleton replica when their gym teacher went to the bathroom. She'd sat in the back of the classroom, feet tight in her old shoes, and she'd smiled and smiled.

With a drawn-out sigh, Marvin pointed at the strange woman standing beyond the glass. "Look down," he said.

Grace followed her new friend's command. First, she noted the white dress flats, the footwear shining like lacquered snow. *Who'd wear those shoes at a hospital?*

"A nurse," she whispered, answering her own question.

The shoes were the giveaway.

Any adult-sized passersby took in a sweet-faced, cowed woman in a salmon-colored sweatshirt.

Nothing to see.

But kids would see. Masked, unmasked, it didn't much matter.

The Children *did* see.

Then, the trio's gaze rose as one to observe the woman's protruding belly. From a curve at the mid-section, something pushes against the pockets. Almost like she was pregnant.

*Except it's not sitting right.*

When the thing inside the woman's shirt punched and kicked against the cloth material, Grace gasped. Her hand flew to her mask, to her bird face. She winced when the razor-sharp beak sliced open her palm. Blood splattered onto the cement. Dark red droplets fat and singular like cherry-pie filling.

"She's got a baby in there," Grim said, stating the more than obvious.

Marvin nodded.

But then, silence. More hesitation. Standing on either side of the girl in the bird mask, the boy in the dog mask, and the other child in their skull mask waited.

Grace wiped her bloody fingers across the front of her dress. She smeared a crude circle, then a star. She didn't check her handiwork, operating by feeling alone.

"We must save the child," she said. Her declaration was loud and profane. Like the raucous trill of a raven. She pressed her still-bleeding hand against the sliding glass door. With a heavy whooshing sigh, it slid open for her. Before Marvin could protest or Grim could applaud Grace's sudden decisive action, she was gone. On the other side of the glass, heading toward the nurse and the baby secreted away inside her sweatshirt.

***

Back at headquarters, the Director stood at rigid attention, waiting for the report to come from the three members sent into the field. The rookie in her bird mask and the other two—"the outcasts among the outsiders," as so many of the other Children called them. The Director would sigh if capable of doing so. But time left them stiff with age, always silent unless throwing their voice out wide to issue commands or reprimand or on the rare occasion offer praise.

The Society's latest mission proved a tricky undertaking for everyone. Not only were the operatives meant to prevent a new member from joining the ranks of the Society prematurely and/or inadvertently, but the Director received hints regarding potential sensitive information related to one of the Children selected for the mission. One of *their* Children.

"Stay inside the mission parameters," they'd warned the trio.

Of course, the Director understood the compulsion to disobey, to look deeper for the monsters. After all, they were a child once. Lost like all these others. Unlike these new Children, when the Director founded the American chapter, disguises went further than mere masks or glamours.

They remember running through the trees, bare feet covered in the dirt of a new world. A baptism in reverse. They recall darkness settling over the land their people tried to break. The world was unwilling to yield and was still imbued with enough power to fight back against trespassers.

Then, everyone disappeared. And the Director found themselves hidden in a tree. Not *up* in a tree, but inside. Living, but unseen by all who followed.

And there they stayed until there wasn't much difference between the Child in the Tree and the wood of the tree itself. Then, someone felled the tree and sanded it down, making a door from the tree. The door was the Child. The Child, the door. In subsequent years, they became the Director of the Secret Society of Schrödinger's Children.

On one side of the door, the Children gathered, taking orders, giving reports of the world outside. On the other side, the craftsman who'd changed the tree and the Child into a door left a word carved, marking the hiding place no one who came after ever guessed.

One word: "CROATOAN."

***

Another nurse stopped the three Children, blocking their way forward once they'd made it inside the hospital. Unsure how to respond when the woman leaned forward, her "cheerful, yet wary in the way grown-ups always are of children they don't know" face close to the feathers, her lipstick-glazed mouth appearing like candle wax set in stasis, Grace looked to her companions. Forgetting how much emotion the masks hid, she was unable to gauge a proper response from their reactions. Or lack thereof.

"Well, it's early for Halloween. But y'all sure have some darlin' costumes."

Grace nodded. Over and over again. Through the compact lens magnification of her birds' eyes, she tracked the other nurse. The one with the baby hidden under her shirt. The other woman paced back and forth. Grace caught her eyeing the exit. Something between the growl of an empty stomach and the lightheaded sensation of euphoria took hold of the girl.

But they'd need to get closer for confirmation.

"You lost?"

Grace stopped nodding.

"We're looking for our..." Marvin's words came in choked gritty sobs. Like he spoke through six feet of soil. Maybe less.

"...aunt," Grim finished.

The interrogating nurse nodded this time, standing up straight. Her eyes focused on a tiny corner of the ceiling. Weighing the value of the Children's words against her belief.

Grace exhaled. Her breath caused the feathers to fluff up around her cheeks. She pointed over to the nurse in the pink sweatshirt. The one with a secret. The one with a hand pulled inside the sleeve of her shirt, covering the gurgles and gasps of her "secret."

"There," Grace said.

"There? Oh."

Grace took the other nurse's hand, and her companions followed. They stayed close to Grace and her escort, but not too close.

"Marie? Hey, hon, you waiting around for some kids?"

But the other nurse's words went unheeded as the nurse in pink made a sudden dash for the sliding glass doors. Her face transformed into an anguished mask of its own. Mouth downturned, eyes wide and streaming tears—a Tragedy mask come to life. One hand, with bloody cuticles, chewed open so thin streaks of pink blood remained behind, pressed against the other nurse's wrist, twisting her around. Soon enough, the smiling nurse took to screaming. Letting everyone know her pain.

All the eyes, young and old, turned to take in the scene playing out across the hospital lobby. The weeping woman trying to make her escape. Her stomach appeared alive with wriggling limbs. Down at the Children's eye level, they caught the impression of a face pressing against the soft pink fabric. The muffled, choked cries followed.

The nurse in pink looked up, staying focused on the sliding doors.

But by staying so keyed in and focused, she missed the skull-masked boy and the dog-masked boy as each put a tiny leg out—across her path. The slightest contact proved good enough. Her arms flew up and her body tilted forward, the angle unsustainable for balance.

Grace put her hands out. Always so tiny. A child's hands.

But nothing so small as those on the naked screeching newborn dropped the short distance from the loosened folds of the nurse's pink sweatshirt into Grace's arms. The shock knocked the wind from the screaming baby. The girl pulled the baby close, getting it as far away from the nurse as possible. She held the shivering infant against her, feeling a heartbeat through near-translucent skin.

*Time's passing. But what is Time when you're either alive or dead, or neither alive nor dead?*

Grace looked down at the baby. Still silent, but alive. Breathing returned to normal with each slow exhale. The remnants of an eggshell-colored mask melted away like cotton candy in a cup of water, dissolved to nothing but a sweet aftertaste.

*Still alive though. Still breathing.*

A hand, a tiny, tiny hand, scrawny like a bird's leg, shot up to brush against Grace's mask. His thin, new fingers touched her feathers.

A voice spoke inside of Grace. A voice from behind the bird mask and from behind her *Grace* mask as well.

*I know you.*

Then, hands took the baby away from her. "He's okay," someone said.

*Good.*

Marvin and Grim helped Grace back on her feet. They offered no condolences or reassurances.

But, then she heard the voice again...

***

By the time the detectives finished interviewing Barbara, it was close to the end of the day. They'd asked her all kinds of questions from every angle. *Did she know Marie St. Anna? Did she suspect her colleague capable of stooping so low as to steal someone else's child? Was she aware of what a brave thing she'd done, confronting Marie and saving the poor baby boy? What compelled her to act?*

Barbara kept silent about the children in the masks. No one else said anything about them anyway. The police never asked her about them. Such a strange detail to leave unremarked upon.

During the barrage of questions, Barbara sensed their words crowding her and her heart beat fit to wake the devil. She almost asked, "But what about the Children..." But she held her words, letting them sit heavy on her tongue.

Then, she swallowed them back.

One of the officers left his card. A young man. Well-built, chiseled features, like an old movie star. Barbara blushed when she took the card. She was old enough to be his mother.

Leaving the administrator's office, Barbara paused. She carried all her belongings with her. After all, she'd been about to leave when the..."incident"...occurred. Now, she'd walk out the sliding doors, go home to draw a bath and finish one of the old TV Guide crosswords she'd saved up over the years. One referencing shows starring forgotten names like James Garner, Suzanne Somers, or Michael Landon.

But not yet. Something kept her there. She poked her head back in the office and cleared her throat to get the handsome young detective's attention. "Excuse me," she said. "The child. The baby. Is he..."

"He'll be fine, ma'am," the boy detective said. "I believe the infant's back in the...nursery."

Barbara nodded, appreciating the delicacy of his phrasing. She hadn't worked in the neonatal unit for years. But word got around. Especially with special cases. "Yes, yes, the mother, she's..."

***

"It's me," Grace said, standing on her tip-toes to look through the thin pane of glass in the door.

Through the glass, she glimpsed a hospital room and a hospital bed. She watched another version of herself, blonde hair spread across a pillow in an angel's halo. No bird mask, but an oxygen mask strapped across the bottom of her face and a long tube snaking down inside of her. Even with the mask, Grace knew herself. After all, she'd watched a video of herself sleeping before. Stuck in a fog of deep, deep sleep. So deep she'd never wake up, no matter what happened or who entered the room. So deep she wouldn't feel a thing.

Marvin tugged on her elbow, trying to get her attention. "Come on, Grace, let's go," he said.

"Wait, wait," she said. "One more thing."

But this was "one more thing" of many.

First, she'd followed the doctors and nurses taking the baby to get checked out after the rescue. Everyone credited the nurse and said nothing of the Children. Marvin told her their mission was over and they needed to go. But she wanted to watch as the doctors and nurses looked and listened all over. Like a pawnbroker assessing the value of an heirloom sacrificed.

No one noticed the Children. The bird mask, the dog mask, and the skull mask were background detail, like the paneled ceilings and track lighting, tiny colorful footprints painted from a stencil along the wall. As easy for the adults in the room to ignore the odors of lollipops and ammonia.

Grace sobbed when the doctor—the one who looked like he was in charge—said the baby was okay. When she turned to her companions, Marvin looked down, avoiding her gaze and the thick black circles of Grim's mask hid their eyes from view, offering no clue to their response.

She followed the nurses down winding hospital corridors, skipping between the cracks in the checkerboard pattern on the floor.

*What'd Daddy say about Mama?*

*She flew the coop.*

'Guess that makes you the Mama now.'

She followed the baby and his white-garbed escort to the nursery. She ignored Marvin's pleas, even as they grew louder and more insistent. "Remember what the Director said."

Grace recalled a door. A closed door. Nothing good ever came from behind closed doors. Too many secrets.

She no longer cared for the dog-masked boy. Grim, on the other hand. Silent, aspiring to danger, letting her go. She felt the sudden urge to stick her beak through the black eye sockets of his mask. To indulge in decay and melancholy. Pull out a wriggling graveyard worm and share it with Grim, each swallowing down their half.

They put the baby boy into one of the fiberglass bassinets, with his naked form wrapped tight in a rainbow-striped blanket.

Grace followed them down another hall and then another.

"Poor baby. Too much trauma for such a young child. Hope he gets the help he needs or finds some family to help him."

"Mmhmm. His mama still in the coma ward?"

"Mmm."

In the coma ward, outside a room with a closed door, the name on the chart belonged to a "Jane Doe." A made-up name. A disguise. Masking the truth of who the comatose girl was.

Grace brought her feet back flat on the floor. She touched her mask.

"I'm still here," she said.

Grim answered. Beneath her mask, Grace's cheeks flushed at their attention. "It doesn't matter if you know. Doesn't change anything. It only matters if...*they* know."

Grace wanted to reach up and rip the skull mask and the dog mask off her companions' faces. Then, she'd do the same for the bird mask over her face. She wondered what she'd find under there. An oxygen mask? A smile? Tears? Was her skin torn away, replaced with feathers and glue and string?

"Fine," she said. "Let's go home."

She opened the hospital room door and her companions followed. On the other side, the Children hummed and buzzed with Society work. The potential for something better lifted their spirits. Grace watched everything and changed.

Not all at once, but slowly. Day by day, moment by moment. Until she couldn't recognize herself any other way.

# Two Rare Specimens

The closet door opens onto a picture-perfect recreation of the twins' old childhood bedroom. The monster emerges from the darkness, from somewhere beyond the closet's interior. But before the creature's slimy tentacles drag across the shag carpeting, before its pale humanoid hands—soft and squishy to the touch, like wet play-dough with in-grown black nails at the tips—tear plaster chunks from the wall and make demonic shadow puppets, an alarm is triggered.

The monster's red eyes, always bleeding in their natural state, open wider than ever before. Its pupils double, then triple in size when the floodlights blast through the black. They're projected from across the span of the mock room, capturing the creature in their glow.

The first of the twin brothers, older by a full five minutes, speaks from behind the shield wall of fluorescence. "Hello again. We hoped you'd come."

The monster lunges forward, stabbing its sharpened fingernails deep into the nearest lump hidden under Star Wars sheets. Its jaw unhinges to reveal teeth the same ebony tint as its nails. Each tooth comes to a sharpened point, but they're also serrated on their sides. Like someone converted old Indian arrowheads into dentures. Regardless, claws and teeth alike come away with a gelatinous substance coating them, instead of the anticipated gore, blood, and viscera of a devoured child.

The beast straightens, sliding forward on its mass of tentacles. A loose black trench coat stretches across its upper body. But when it moves, the cloth slides away revealing a squirming mass of cephalopodic limbs, turning the monster into a many-phallused pervert flashing elementary school playgrounds.

Every instinct tells the monster to run from the light, to retreat to the cold, dark embrace of the shadows in the closet.

The second twin, younger by five minutes, speaks next. "You've ingested a heavy sedative. Heavy enough even for you. Please don't try and fight."

The monster remembers what waits past the light: there's a door with a poster—cartoon soldiers or robots capable of changing into trucks or guns. Except that's not true this time. The monster's failed to account for the passage of time since the pheromones and sweet fear scents of children waited behind this particular closet door. Inside the rectangular storage space, time is meaningless. For the monster in the closet, there's simply time to wait on one side of the door and time to scare on the other.

But those boys, it remembers those boys…and then realizes how they no longer sound like boys. Secrets from their shared past flood the monster's mind. It's too far away to draw strength from the immeasurable void of the closet in which it thrives. The twins—they've tricked him. Two men—grown men—now wait for the monster. They wear jeans and khaki shirts with the sleeves rolled up. Their arms are hairy, except where they display blue and green inked tattoos or where veins show through tough and leathery skin. However much time's passed, these two have taken it harder than most.

The monster gags, both from finding the twins grown and as a last-ditch effort to free itself from the effects of whatever poison it's ingested. But no gorge rises from inside its bottomless pit of a stomach. It's fed on the memories of nightmares for too long.

Its eyelids grow heavy, falling like theater curtains cut loose from their bindings. The monster's limbs become like gelatin with poison filling its system, polluting it. Rendering it wobbly and inconsequential.

One of the twins pulls out a two-way radio. "Security, prepare for extraction of the specimen. Ladies and gentlemen, we've got ourselves a boogeyman."

It's difficult for the monster to hear past its own moaning and defiant cries soon reduced to pitiful mewlings, but it swears it hears something like applause.

***

Twenty years earlier: the same room. The same beds. The carpet, the posters, and the door are back as well. And the twins are young boys, small and frightened, each sitting under their science fiction bedsheets, shivering. Their father's in boxer shorts and shirt sleeves, sweating. He slurs his speech after pounding a few Coors. "Boys, how many times I gotta tell y'all. There ain't no boogeyman, no monster in the closet."

The oldest speaks first. Teeth chattering, a trickle of blood dribbles down his chin from where he's bitten his lip. "B-b-but, wuh-wuh-we sa-sa-saw it, d-d-d-daddy."

The younger twin nods his head. Not saying anything. The lower half of his face reveals a mess of tears, snot, and spit. Their father considers the boy and rolls his eyes. "Fuckin' pussies," he mutters to himself.

The man stomps through the bedroom doorway, making a beeline for the closet. Its handle fills his meaty paw, before he wrenches the door open.

There's no boogeyman, no nightmare creature bred to scare boys and girls, to feed off fear or flesh—depending on its mood. There's nothing but board games, old stuffed animals scented by baby-soft skin and mothballs, and the twins' clothes—all matching outfits purchased by their mother. The newest ones are worn thin, bunching up where they've gone too tight. But what can the twins do? Their daddy won't let anyone buy them nice things anymore. He says he needs the money for his *medicine*.

His medicine comes in twelve-packs and glass bottles most days.

There's something else inside the closet. Darkness. Shadows. The overall absence of light.

The boogeyman hides in the spaces between shadows, laughing with a throaty chuckle as its too-thick tongue marinates in its bloody mouth juices. The father rants and raves, his back to the open closet now. Oblivious to the malevolent presence waiting *right...behind...him.* "Goddammit. Nothing there. Nothing there but more nothing. Buncha crap your mother insists on spoiling you little shits with. What does Hank get, huh? I get anything from that bitch, huh? That *whore*?"

A tiny voice cuts through the noise of two worlds, the twins speak as one. "Where's Mama?"

In between the shadows, the boogeyman cuts its laughter short. The question's a good one. Their mother usually follows. Their mother comes as peacemaker, pulling the father away. But where's she gone?

There's a moment of hesitation on the creature's part, its glamour flickering. The father's eye locks on one of the creature's blood-spewing orb. "The hell..."

***

Electric jolts course through the boogeyman's prone form, as he's strapped to an otherwise bare slate-gray table. The twins wear pine-green scrubs and face shields over their visages. Thick vulcanized rubber gloves cover their hands. The creature writhes against its restraints, hissing, spitting.

One brother steps to a nearby control panel. Like something out of Dr. Frankenstein's laboratory in the movies. The twin's hand rests on a knob for a moment. Then, he turns the power higher. The monster's blood boils under its wrinkled skin, the liquid popping and bursting inside. Bubbling black from open wounds like the twins struck oil from within the boogeyman's hideous form.

"Think he's had enough, Ethan?" the younger one asks.

The older one nods, "I think he has, Ian." The one named Ethan pulls back on the electric charge. The boogeyman spasms once, twice. Then, it falls still against the hard surface of the operating table.

The creature runs through a catalog of voices, a jukebox of impressions it's amassed over the years, intended to mislead, intimidate, and terrify. Its jaw aches, so it settles for smiling on the inside when it makes what it believes is a perfect choice. "Fuckin' pussies," it says, speaking in their father's voice, "Long time no see, boysssssss."

The hiss at the end's not like a snake's, it's more an unpinned gas grenade. Some trench warfare relic spewing poison in the air.

A black-gloved fist slams into the monster's mouth, jagged teeth falling into the abyss of its throat. The brother named Ian pulls his hand out, digits coated in monster spittle. He makes a shushing motion, green and yellow snot-slime slaloming around his finger. "Cute," he says.

The boogeyman twists its head to the side or at least as close as possible, given the restraining straps around its forehead and neck. The creature spits the jagged shards of its teeth out. Already new crooked, ebony replacements slice their way up through its bleeding gums.

"Thought we'd finished with each other," the creature says.

"Yeah, me too," Ian replies.

Ethan puts a hand on his twin's shoulder, pulling his brother away from the monster. A look passes between the two. Even though the exam room lights hurt its eyes, the boogeyman takes note. A monster's survival depends on noticing such moments. Signs of potential weakness, something to exploit later.

When the time's right.

"Circumstances changed," Ethan says, picking up the baton from his twin.

The boogeyman says nothing. Acting like it's learned its lesson. Acting like it's chastised and will play the good little monster.

"How much do you know about the monster under the bed?"

This time, the monster responds in its own voice. Sounding like a million damned souls screaming at once but set to a higher frequency so it's akin to nails on a chalkboard, the record player needle scratched against vinyl played at two times speed. "Oh," it says, "You boysssssss fucked up."

***

Before the twins and the boogeyman have any mutual business to consider *finished*, their father locks eyes with the monster and spits into the darkness. A yellow wad of phlegm meant to splatter against the back wall instead gets lost in the abyss. Still, the boogeyman stands its ground, waiting patiently and keeping as much of itself in the in-between realm of shadows from which it emerged as it's able.

"Goddamn, got a fuckin' raccoon in there or something..." The father's eyes, bloodshot and rheumy, drift away from whatever mystery his children's closet holds. Making fists. Behind his back, the twins use their secret sign language to communicate.

*"Mom."*

*"No. Mom."*

*"What?"*

*"Monster?"*

*"Monster."*

"What the hell are y'all doing, waving your hands around?"

A silence passes between the boys. A silence as brief and insubstantial as anything. But for the twins, it's a silence imbued with every moment of their lives—past, present, and whatever the future holds.

"Well, answer me."

Ethan takes the lead. He speaks for himself and his brother. "You can take him," he says. "We won't tell anyone and they wouldn't believe us anyway. We'll take the blame. Just please...take him."

Their father scratches his head with one hand and his balls with the other. "What the hell you talkin' about, son? Swear, y'all are like your Mama. You're always talking, talking. Getting me all confused..."

If the twins note the tears streaming down their old man's face at this moment, neither's features acknowledge it. In truth, they will only look at the man they've called "father" with greater and greater reluctance each passing day in their shared Hell. The darkness in the closet spills into the half-light of their bedroom. It comes with a strong scent of black licorice, enough to make all three humans cough.

Their father continues his weepy monologue, ignoring or too drunk to notice the sudden change in their environment. "I showed her though. She ain't talkin' no more. No, sir. Maybe it's time I show you, too."

But before he shows his progeny anything, the father feels the sticky suction cups beneath the boogeyman's tentacle, as it wraps around his neck and the bottom half of his face. Cutting words and breath off at once.

The father's eyes widen.

And then, the boogeyman takes him.

***

The phosphorescent appearance of a young girl's bedroom and belongings under blacklights gives objects like doll babies, stuffed animals, pink frilly curtains, and princess bedsheets an eerie glow. Like the creatures living at the bottom of an ocean trench. The boogeyman blinks its eyes, trying to keep them moisturized. Already its tongue's become a scratchy sandpaper brick inside its mouth. It's (as close as a wicked creature gets to) grateful for the twins' having replaced the normal lighting with these blacklights, an effort meant to replicate the living darkness in which it thrives.

But it's been away from the closet too long. Already its strength's sapped from its limbs. Already there's a rattle in its speech, like the burr of the cicada reborn from a dried-out husk.

"Is thisss where she wasssss taken?"

Ian nods. Ever since the boogeyman made his feelings known about the likelihood of anyone or anything (including itself) surviving an encounter with the creature known as "the monster under the bed," the younger twin's stayed quiet. Damn near monosyllabic, even as his brother's made rough attempts at jovial bonding and encouragement.

The boogeyman appreciates the fear radiating off the younger brother. And not just because of how delicious it smells. But also because it's justified.

His tasty fear's almost strong enough to distract the monster from the strange gear worn by the twins. Black catsuits with cybernetic enhancements integrated into the fabric. Blue lights flash and spark along arms and legs. The helmets over their faces make their features appear to swim behind the yellow glass of their face shields. They tell him it's the latest in cyber-occult tactical gear, and claim it's capable of withstanding the pressures of the darkness from which monsters like the boogeyman come.

It's happy to let them believe that.

The suits stimulate the muscles of their wearers and raise their body temperatures to the level of a walking fever. The twins move on tip-toes without any apparent pain. Their shoulders hunch against their ears. Through the face-shield glass, their lips pull back into rictus grins. When they speak, their words come in a throaty rattle like the boogey-man's voice.

"Can you open the gateway under her bed?" Ian asks.

As far as inquiries go, it's a formality, and the boogeyman knows it. After everything the twins went through, there's no way the pair intend to leave anything to chance. Especially nothing involving bringing *it* back from their old bedroom closet, fulfilling a vow made years ago and sealed in blood.

*So much blood.*

***

Back in their old bedroom on the night that entwined their fate to the boogeyman's, the twins appear shocked by the amount of blood their father contained. The boogeyman's not surprised. It's tapped an adult skin suit before and drank to the lees enough times, gorging itself on life-giving serum, so it knows how filling the contents of one brutal, loutish forty-something can be.

One pale hand rubs the taut gray flesh of its bloated belly.

"What comessss next?" it asks the silent duo, as they watch the creature clean their father's internal organs from the suckers on its tentacles.

Simpatico, the twin boys point to the open closet door. "Go back. We'll tell them we did it. They won't believe us at first. But they'll believe more in us than in you," Ethan says, repeating some of the points made earlier.

The boogeyman nods. He slides across the carpeted floor. "What'ssssss to stop me from killing you both. Getting a complete ssssset."

Ian gets the last word, making a promise that takes his brother by surprise. "Leave us tonight in exchange for...what we've given you. But if y-y-you ever find us in this room, waiting on the other side of your closet...you can come for us."

***

"You make deals like devils," the creature from the closet tells the younger twin. "Always finding a way to get what you want."

"Huh?" Ian's eyes resemble his brother's so bloodshot they appear ready to burst from their sockets. Straining to escape.

The boogeyman's identified the black substance pumping into the twins' suits. He recalls the needles piercing his hide, making their extractions while he writhed on the lab table.

"You think you can handle my essssssence?" it asks with playful malevolence.

But Ian's answer comes with an air of deadly seriousness. "It....it ...hasssss to work." He coughs, a tiny crimson blood splatter popping against his face shield like burst bubble gum. He turns to his brother. "Ethan. Are we ready?"

The older twin holds an electronic tablet and uses a stylus to check off items. Like he's grocery shopping. His gloves are sticky with a black tarry resin. It's the substance used to mark the summoning circle on the white shag rug beside the little girl's bed. *His niece.*

The boogeyman tilts up a portrait framed in silver. But not real silver, as its skin remains untainted by the exposure. A little girl—a playful scowl with her front teeth missing. "She lookssssss like her grandfather..."

Before the boogeyman completes its observation, Ian lunges from the bookshelves where he's waited and lands a wild punch into the folds of the creature's stomach. The monster's belching cough should make a human quiver with fear, the assaulting effect too much for a homo sapiens' systems to process. The suits appear to work though. The younger twin stands his ground. Indeed, he wraps a heavy hand around the squishy folds of the creature's neck, immune to the paralyzing slimes excreted from the boogeyman's pores.

The boogeyman gets the message. He snaps off a salute. "Sssssir, yesssir."

By the bed, Uncle Ethan takes the lead and lifts the side of a frilled bedspread from the floor. He clears his throat, making a sound like a strangling cat. When the boogeyman turns his attention to the bed, the man gestures for the creature to go first. To head into the darkness under the bed "After you," he says.

The brothers' gear includes rappelling ropes and guide lines, the terminus of the lines falling somewhere out of sight. The boogeyman's not afforded a spot on the rope. It'll free solo into the lair of the monster under the bed. Again, the message is clear: No one's protecting the boogeyman.

And it's not surprised.

"Yessss. I ssssssuppossssse that'sss the way of it."

***

After the boogeyman leaves, the brothers wait by the front door of a house they'll never live in again. Never sleep in again. They hold their mother's phone, sticky with her blood, between their hands. The police come first and then the ambulances. Then, the social workers and insomniac crime-beat reporters up late listening to the police-band radio hoping for juicy rumors of violence. When these strangers with sympathetic faces find the mother, the story unfolds as expected. *The abusive husband going too far. The two children left without the parent who cared for them.*

But when these others reach the twins' room and discover the father's remains, the narrative changes, descending into chaos. Whatever sympathies they hold for the boys are drained away. It's not disgust or shock, but something beyond—a numbing to prepare their consciences for what follows.

There's nothing as far as human reactions go to explain the atrocious slaughter in the bedroom. It's a level of unsettling akin to watching a hamster devour its young. It's not something any—well, most—humans could understand off-hand.

The boys lock themselves into an amusement park ride with a steep, inadvisable downward trajectory, building momentum as they go. Seconds become hours become days, weeks, and years.

A trial follows, in which the boys confess to murdering their father. They refuse to take the blame for their mother's death; however, the gruesomeness of their father's slaying makes it near impossible for anyone to believe they acted in self-defense. Jurors consider the arrangement of limbs spelling out foul expletives across their Lego collection and comic books and assume a level of premeditation behind the violence.

If they're going to take the blame for dear old dad's departure, then they must do the same for their mother. Never mind their father's fingerprints on the shattered Evan Williams bottle or the glittering glass pieces embedded in her skull fragments.

They're tried as adults. But they avoid a life sentence. It's the judge's and prosecution's idea of compromise. Sending two boys with quiet faces and thin bodies like a memory into gen pop at one of the toughest prisons in the state. For good or ill, they come with a reputation.

They don't need to earn one out in the prison yard. But they fight day after day, year after year, to keep their rep—to live up to the expectations of those anticipating bloodthirsty murderers and unhinged savagery. Their fellow inmates recognize a coldness, a lack of humanity in the eyes of these children. No matter what story one believes, it's clear the pair lost more than their parents on the night in question.

A gang leader, an eccentric type who runs things behind bars and has a penchant for misfits, takes a shine to the boys. But he keeps them at arms' length, never so close as to consider them "under his wing." He mentions how the twins stared into darkness more intense than anything they'd face behind bars. He assures them the dark's a limitless resource and as long as they're connected to it—they'll survive.

Time passes. Then, they're free. Not only do they return to the outside world, but they emerge with a fortune inherited from a long-dead relative—though the specifics of the relationship and the inheritance remain shrouded in a thick veil of secrecy. No one recalls any rich aunts or uncles on the family tree, and no one knows what happened to the gang leader who taught them everything. He's disappeared from inside the prison without a trace. But no one cares enough about the young men to put those two disparate pieces together. So there's no one left to ask where the old gangbanger's hidden fortune went. The one he spoke about all the time, the stash of a lifetime hidden somewhere he'd only divulge on his deathbed.

***

Even with their occult-enhanced suits and the boogeyman's blood pumping through their veins, the twins don't take too well to the dimensional shift in perspective when they slip under Ian's daughter's bed. The boogeyman wonders if what he said before diving headfirst through the open gateway made any impact on the overall mood.

"If there'sssss anything to find it'sssssss her bonessssss. The monster under the bed doesn't take hossstagessss. It takessss snackssss."

In a world of shadows, it's easier to hide in the light. The monster from the closet motions for the green-in-the-gills brothers to follow, leading them in bounding leaps from one sliver of pale illumination to the next. The twins keep turning their heads after every jump, moving like something else is out there.

"Other bedsssss," the boogeyman says, offering the bare minimum of explanation for the disembodied voices floating in the ether.

*"There's nothing under the bed, sweetie."*

*"I already checked…"*

*"Now, go to sleep."*

*"Shut up! Shut up! Stop fucking crying…!"*

The boogeyman stops when one of the twins grabs it by the shoulder. It's Ethan, the older one, pulling the monster's pale, pulsing body against his own form vibrating with adrenaline and chthonic energy. The boogeyman beams, revealing a complete set of re-grown teeth. Taunting and tempting the man—one of the boys who got away—to knock them out all over again.

Seeing red trickle down the human's cheeks from bleeding eyes, the boogeyman wonders how its serum will affect them the longer they're pumping it through their bodies—what might the consequences be? "How clossssssse are we?" Ethan hisses, his face appearing to collapse in on itself as he strains to get each word out.

The boogeyman swallows back the urge to tease or to go further and spit in the face of his captor. "Not far now."

Ian raises a hand, signaling for the others to catch up to his position in a spot of inky blackness. Under the beds, there's no way to tell if younger Ian's inches or millions of miles ahead of his trailing companions. He's taken to moving through the nightmare realm much better than his brother. His body swims in the ethereal soup of the void. Up, down, side to side, inside out. It's as though he's stripped away more humanity than the level-headed, natural leader Ethan. Like he's already lost enough to let the rest go for a song.

***

Ian holds the girl in the rocking chair where he's finished her nightly allotment of fairy-tale stories. She's fallen asleep, snuggled between his chest and stomach. A dribble of milk from her bottle rests on her chin. Golden hair, pink cheeks from the final teeth emerging. Ian whisper-sings a lullaby to her. Something about black sheep and the demands made on their wool.

Ethan, the visiting uncle who's stayed for longer than Ian expected, sighs from the open doorway to the nursery. Ian looks up from the rocking chair and returns a weary nod to his "big" brother. He stands, holding the baby girl against his body. Then, he sets her on her princess bed and plants a bristly kiss on her forehead.

Under the shadows, she squirms. Hands slap against the fitted sheet of her bed. Closing around the cloth, then opening again. Like something's pulling at her from under the bed, but she's trying her damnedest to fight back. Ian scans the room, looking over the built-in shelves and the locked wardrobe. There's no closet in the room—by design. There are no closets anywhere in the house. Giving the dark room a satisfied nod, he moves to join his brother in the hallway.

Neither counts the shadows stretched across the bedroom floor. So they miss the extra one, creeping, stretching into the sliver of moonlight stabbed across the pale floor.

When the door closes, the child's scream sounds short and cold. It's a shiv of melting ice in the twins' backs.

Ethan throws the door open, wishing to save his "baby" brother from the pain. As a result, he's the one to see the girl's face under the bed, the tears in her eyes. A look of disbelief he wishes his own mirrored.

When she's gone, Ethan drags his screaming twin from the room. His brother pulls at his shirt and slams his fists against the closed nursery door. But Ethan won't budge, won't relent to the desperate, gibbering pleas. "She's gone," he says, though he knows it's not enough.

Ian slumps to the floor. A broken, hollowed-out man.

Ethan's heart—whatever remains of it—breaks to observe his brother in such a state. After everything they've suffered, the sight of the other he's shared his entire existence with brought low is enough to send both spiraling into states of mind they believed long behind them.

Ian picks himself up from the hallway floor and this initial hopelessness engendered by second contact with the world of monsters.

No tears appear on his face. There's only the darkness. Always the darkness.

"We need to contact...it. The thing from our closet. It'll help us."

"But it'll kill us."

"Unless..."

***

Until now, the boogeyman's never encountered the monster under the bed. No delusions of unity exist between the creatures of the void as there are with human beings. So, the boogeyman's reaction to encountering this other monstrous being, this child of the black, is fresh—freed from any expectation of kinship. The monster under the bed slithers across the void on its long serpentine body. Taloned hands flail near a head made of sharp angles. Bulbous growths riddle its limbs, neck, and armored body segments. Inside these heavy tumorous pods, a gray slurry sloshes against the pink membrane. Whatever's inside these sacs becomes impenetrable to the prying eyes of the trio watching. The boogeyman estimates each pod is the approximate size of a small child though.

It admires the storage method employed by the other monster. The mutual respect of one hunter paying silent singular tribute to another.

There's nowhere to hide in the place under the beds. It's what the boogeyman tried to communicate to the brothers before they dove into the darkness, but the message never got through. So, it's not surprising they're both so stunned, lost and directionless as the monster under the bed appears before them.

First, there's nothing. Then, there's a monster.

"Eileen!"

Ian charges through the darkness, toward the misshapen form of the monster under the bed. The boogeyman makes no effort to stop him. *If this child-man wants to kill himself over his young when the whelp's already dead, then who am I to stand in the way?*

It doesn't expect the monster under the bed to respond to the name of the man's daughter. After all, the boogeyman's got no recollection of the names of those it's either frightened or feasted upon over its many years of existence.

The man who makes a fire doesn't recall every tree used for kindling after all. He takes what's needed for his survival.

So, it's surprising when the worm-like monster pivots to face the charging brother-father. The creature's mouth opens with its lower jaw bifurcating and insectile pedipalps swallowing up the emptiness between the charging man and itself.

The boogeyman doesn't look into its fellow monster's eyes or quivering mouthparts. As a fear-feeder, its instinct is to seek out the juiciest repositories of terror. On the monster under the bed, one of the pods hums and glows orange with a fear signature calling out in a siren's song. The slimy flesh retracts, peeled back like an open blister. There's a girl inside and she's glowing.

She's the one who's afraid.

"What'sssssss wrong with her?"

The boogeyman doesn't ask why the little girl reacts with such fear...to the looming presence of her *father*. Rather than to the monster. If anything, in a split second of observation, the boogeyman grows more and more certain young Eileen's trying to burrow deeper *inside* the monster under the bed. She shudders as Ian calls her again. "Eileen!" Orange afterbirth-like offal slakes from the monster's wound, splattering against and disappearing *into* the void.

Still, the open sac pulses like a warning light.

"But no, it'sssssss...."

The boogeyman turns in time to catch the black and yellow claws bursting through the gloves worn by older twin Ethan. The spotting pattern on the bestial talons reminds the boogeyman of overripe banana peels. But there's nothing mushy or rotting inside those sudden solid sharp growths. They come fast, slicing across the boogeyman's face, pulling the monster's loose doughy skin so its features sit askew on its skull. Like a child's art project hung crooked on a refrigerator door by a too-busy parent.

A high-pitched keening wail follows, sounding like the screams of the damned. White flashes of light explode in the boogeyman's peripheral vision, like paparazzi cameras snapping a million not-so-surreptitious photos all at once. *Pop-pop-pop.*

*pop-pop-pop-pop-pop-pop-pop.*

Now it's the boogeyman's turn to get lost in a void that's the chromatic opposite of the one in which it thrives. It's bathed in white light. Up and down, backward and forward—all become meaningless distinctions. As the monster passes out, its hands and tentacles wipe away wet, sticky chunks of organic matter. There's a chill running down the boogeyman's form—a realization of what's happened and of how wrong everything's been since it emerged from the twins' closet door.

The girl is a bomb. Or she's got a bomb sewn inside of her. The boogeyman lacks the time or inclination to make distinctions. All it knows is that the girl is no daughter to mourn. She's bait, an irresistible morsel for the monster under the bed. Now, she's gone and so is the monster. And so are all the other children, lost forever, having been stored inside the beast for later feedings.

*The girl wassssss bait for it. And it wassssss bait for...me.*

***

The boogeyman wakes on what it first believes is another lab table. Except there's something cold and round pressing into its spine. Its head tilts forward, allowing the creature to peer down the length of its body. It finds its chest cavity opened, the flesh pinned back with surgical pins. A black heart beats between a rib cage sundered by a surgical saw. The tubing's stabbed into the fleshy black lump, drawing blood from the source. When the boogeyman's gaze drops lower, a sudden stab of panic takes hold. The monster attempts to wriggle its tentacles but finds them non-responsive. It's paralyzed from the waist down. It wills itself to move, but nothing happens in response.

It's worse than that even. More permanent for one thing. Its limbs aren't frozen or rendered inert. They're gone. Every single one of them.

"You're delicious," Ethan says, holding one of the boogeyman's severed tentacles up to his mouth. His lips glisten, wet with the saltwater and blood, smearing the liquid across his chin in a manner lewd in its presentation. The man's techno-occult suit's stripped away, yet its effects remain visible on his body. The rictus grin and crooked limbs, the fangs and talons. He's stripped nude and the monster he's becoming presses against the seams of his man-flesh.

The boogeyman coughs, watching its heart contract and seeing a surge of black blood shoot through the tubing.

"Take your time," the Ethan-Monster says, between bites of a tentacle.

"Where'sssssss the other?" the boogeyman manages.

"Ian or the....monster under the bed?"

The boogeyman won't answer. It waits for the truth, even as suspicions itch inside its skull, manhandling its brain.

Then, the other twin, Ian, steps into the light. Gore-soaked, naked as his brother, and as monstrous to boot. Blood gushes from his mouth when he speaks, making it hard to pick out his words.

But it doesn't matter. The boogeyman hears the transformed man's voice inside his skull. The twins have gained powers and abilities it takes other monsters lifetimes to develop. "I consumed your 'friend' and brought its power inside me. It's changing me. Soon my skin will melt away and my new scales will show. My legs will fuse and my skin stretch. It'll be beautiful."

"Wasssssss it even your daughter?"

Ethan answers for his younger brother. "It wasssss someone's daughter. Isssssn't that enough?"

The boogeyman makes eye contact with the transforming twin. "And you're eating me?"

The Ethan-Monster nods. Then, he doubles over, clutching the side of the operating table. Except the boogeyman's figured out what the table actually is. Not a table at all. But a door.

*The* door. The entryway to the closet. Or out of it, depending on what side of the door one found themselves on. With it gone, the separation between the world of the twins and the world of darkness disappears.

Crucified to the closet door, the boogeyman strains against the restraints. Flexing its wrists, trying to wiggle them through the tight cuffs. Skin bursts from the strain and more black blood slicks its hands. One hand comes free from the cuffs with a wet crunch.

The brothers laugh, reminding the boogeyman of mockingbirds imitating the birdsong of others. Play-acting, but in a manner good enough so you mistake them for the real thing. Especially if you don't know what to look for.

Still, the boogeyman remains more monster than either of the men. It won't let the pain or fear bubbling up in the pit of its stomach show on its nightmare visage. Instead, it grins. Using its words to mask the true feelings boiling inside. "Sssssuppose that'sssss where the help went then? You eat them up? Or did they run away? Maybe they sssssssssstopped believing in you."

As it speaks, the creature strains to move its mangled fingers, pulling silver pins out. They burn their flesh to the bones. But the boogeyman won't stop.

"Don't you sssssssseeeee what you've done?"

The Ian-Monster slithers closer, its tube-like body slapping against the concrete floor. Trailing the last of its human blood and a mucus secretion squirting like heated honey from pores along its new tail. "What do you mean?"

The boogeyman reaches across his open chest and pulls the other restraints loose. It flops forward like a puppet with a fresh hand up its felt ass.

"Go ahead and try to leave. Try to walk into the light, ssssssseeking whatever revenge or power you believe isssssss yourssssss. Sssssseee how far you get."

The boogeyman shuffles off the closet door. It lands with a wet slap, the severed stumps of its tentacles driven into the hard surface of the floor.

The Ethan-Monster's there. No trace of humanity's left in its coal-black eyes. Regarding the severed boogeyman like an alien assessing its latest abductee. His jaw falls open. And keeps falling, falling, falling.

Until its mouth gapes open like a doorway.

The boogeyman smiles. "Have you two looked at each other? When's the last time you sssssssssssaw your brother?"

But the Ethan-Monster remains locked on the taunting creature at its feet. The Ian-Monster's lowing like some demon cow in heat. Rubbing itself, squeezing secretions onto the floor. Crawling under the makeshift table, disappearing into darkness. The dull gray haze behind the brothers' eyes suggests neither remembers the other.

The boogeyman slithers and slides into the Ethan-Monster's open mouth. Traveling further into the dark. Letting itself be consumed. Until the Ethan-Monster rubs its distended stomach and slithers across the floor on newly-sprung tentacles. Seeking a way out of this space, seeking a doorway.

Hungry for fear.

# The Shark in Her Belly

When Mom returned from her girls' beach weekend, she had a shark growing in her belly. I didn't know this at first. After all, her skin hadn't stretched. Her belly hadn't ballooned, her womb wasn't filling with the viscous saltwater-tainted amniotic fluid through which the shark would swim and feed. The first real outward sign of change came when Mom swore off drinking.

Then, she stopped letting Dad touch her. Both changes happened back to back, shortly after she'd settled in post-vacation.

"My sunburn, babe!" she'd say, eyes rolling back white in her sockets as though some electric shock pumped through her. She wasn't in pain though. Her mouth hung slack, eyelashes fluttering like hummingbird wings in flight. The sight reminded me of people getting healed on the gaudy faith-healer shows I'd watch on Sunday mornings at Grandma's.

Never mind that Mom's skin after vacation didn't look anything like the cooked lobster red of a sunburn but was more of a clam's shell white-to-silver color. When Dad tried to touch her, when he'd caress Mom's silvery, glimmering skin with the tips of his fingers, his hand came back moist, dripping water onto the carpet or the sofa or our dining room table. Mom's skin showed the impression of his fingertips from even the slightest touch, displaying swirling rainbows in the hoops and whorls of Dad's fingerprints.

When Dad got frustrated and stormed off to the garage or the bathroom or to go for a drive, Mom took the opportunity to pull me close, pressing me against her. I tried to get away. "Mommmm, get offa me!" In those moments, it felt like those four words were all I ever said to her.

But she wouldn't listen, wouldn't take no for an answer. She was relentless. I was a "big boy" by then, but not *big-big*. I came up to her belly. She'd lift her shirt and push my ear against the tightening skin. She pushed me so hard that her outie belly button tickled the inside of my ear.

Once the tickling started, laughter followed. Like I'd heard the funniest joke in the world and couldn't restrain my mirth. I'd stop when I heard the ocean inside her.

No lie, I heard waves crashing inside my mother. Breaking against her. No, not *just* waves, not just the rhythmic rise and fall of water controlled by tides and the moon circling above us. A thrashing, splashing sound came next. Something alive moved inside my mother.

When I'd manage to pull myself free, Mom held a finger to her lips. Shushing me. She winked like we'd shared a secret meant only for her, me, and whatever swam inside her.

After the first time Mom held me, I went online and looked up sharks, trying to read everything the SafeSearch on our browser allowed. I started with sharks because I'd heard so much about them in the news while Mom was away with her "girls."

They were all anybody, local news and otherwise, talked about that year. Unless it was war or presidents or diseases, sharks always swam into the spotlight. Dad and I should've found it strange, the way Mom never mentioned sharks when we called her to check in—every night before my bedtime. I pressed my ear against the back of the phone, while Dad held the receiver to the side of his head. I'd listen for the other ladies in the background: Aunt Rachel, Ms. Teena, Laurie Bethel, Mrs. Velvourt, "Cousin" Gary, but I'd only hear water and nothing else. It seemed like Mom took all her calls in the ocean, so even the early morning debriefs sounded as though she'd rolled out of a bed onto the breakers, answering our calls with a curt, sharp-tongued "What?"

The water lapping in Mom's belly reminded me of the sounds picked up on those vacation calls. As though an unsettled presence lingered beside her in the ocean back then and within her body in the present.

In my search for understanding, I learned sharks don't bear their young like humans carry unborn children. Sharks lay eggs. Mom *couldn't* have a shark in her belly. And yet, every fiber of my being from my big toes to my brain screamed at me, loud and insistent, ensuring me *yes, indeed, there was a shark in Mom's belly.*

When bedtime arrived, I turned off the computer and brushed my teeth. The smashed white bristles rubbed against my rounded teeth, nothing too sharp to be found in my jaw. When I finished and went to say goodnight, I found Dad stretched across the living room couch with a wool blanket Grandma had made for us draped over him. I stood on tip-toes to kiss his bristled cheek and he pulled me close, kissing the top of my head.

He smelled like tobacco, but only on his hands, not in his mouth. "Your mom's taking a bath," he told me.

Sometimes grown-ups say things, but they're one-half of a full thought. It's like these brain teasers they share, but they don't tell you where to find the answers in the back of the book. Then, you've got to puzzle out what the problem is *and* the solution as well. And forget about asking follow-up questions! Most times, they'll pretend they don't even know what you're talking about.

Still, what he said sounded straightforward. When I went by Mom and Dad's bathroom, the lights were on. The door was open a crack, a slit cut through the world I knew and understood (most days), to show me something else behind it. Something beyond personal, beyond private, beyond the *grown-up stuff* I'd "understand someday when I was older."

I watched Mom stretched out in the tub. Except I missed seeing the clear surface of the water surrounding her or the slight sheen of soap, dirt, and sweat from her day washed off to encircle her naked body. This water appeared red like someone squeezed paint from the tubes in my art cart to coat the basin of the claw-foot tub. With the water gushing from the spigot, I imagined the red floating to the surface in twisting clouds of crimson. Red. Red like a fire engine, red like flashing lights, red like a warning.

*Red like blood.*

I stood in place while Mom bathed, rubbing her hands up and down her arms, coating her bare skin in the red liquid. She whispered a song or sang in a whisper. Hands moved from her neck to her breasts, then under the blood-red water. She hitched her legs on the sides of the tub. The water sloshed and splashed. Mom slid down, her mouth filling with water, filling with red.

I leaned forward and the floorboard squeaked under my foot. Mom's eyes rolled back. But this time they weren't white. This time, they were black. I ran to my bed and pulled the sheets over my head. Pressed them tight against me. As though I'd cocoon myself in blankets and create an impenetrable force field no one could break or bite through.

With the fuzzy cloth pressed against my ears, blood rushed through my head. This repeating throbbing sound came next, so persistent I worried I'd got something stuck inside me, in my skull. My breathing quickened as I imagined a shark swimming inside, under the bone. Feasting on the pink and gray parts of my brain. This vision over-whelmed my senses

Until all became black.

And then, it was morning.

Dad woke me up late.

He'd never had to wake me up before. Usually, Mom got me through my morning routine. She'd come in singing a silly song about waking up and taking on the day, rhyming words at random. Nonsense stuff. She switched the words around every time and it always made me laugh and laugh. Dad always remained somewhere else in the house, getting ready for work.

But this time, it was Dad with his red tie hanging to his stomach with the end reaching below his belt, looming over my bed like he'd gotten lost and stumbled upon me. Shaving cream remnants decorated his cheeks. "Wake up. We're late!"

No song for me. Nothing to compel me to rise.

But I did all the same.

I got my underwear, socks, and pants on, but still wore my too-small, too-tight pajama shirt, when I stood in the doorway to my room, look-ing out into the hallway and rubbing sleep from my eyes.

"Where's Mom?" I asked.

Dad gave no answer. He walked by with my raincoat—even though it wasn't raining that morning and wasn't supposed to later in the day either. He dropped the coat on me, so it hung loosely from my head. Then, he scooped me up with one hand and held my backpack in his other fist.

His lips were squeezed shut. So tight, the color left them. A low hum escaped, but it wasn't meant for me. More like, he needed to keep a constant sound going long enough to block out something else. Whether it was something he'd taken from the outside world or something trying to escape from inside him, I didn't know. And still don't know.

On the way out the door, without my usual Pop-Tart breakfast from Mom, we passed their bathroom. Its door was closed. Tight this time. Still, I picked up on the water running behind the door. Steam emerged from underneath, curling wisps of white smoky tendrils grabbing for us. Many-limbed, like some squid or octopus.

"Mom?"

Dad kept us moving forward. Didn't stop until he clicked me into my booster seat in the back of the car and we were on our way to school.

I kept my raincoat on all day because my pajama shirt was too small and had cartoon puppies on it. Fine enough for sleeping in, but not something I wanted the other kids to see.

Dad was late to pick me up at the end of the day, too.

Mom remained in the bath when we got home. Stayed in there through dinner and bedtime.

***

This pattern repeated for the rest of the school week. I don't know when, or if, Mom left the bathroom. If she did, it happened when I was in school and Dad was away at work.

Dad didn't take the change too well. At the beginning of the week, he tried showering at the gym, but that soon fell by the wayside. His hair turned curly with sprigs of twirled black like someone other than himself ran their fingers through it, teasing it out. Given the shimmer on the top of his head, I imagined this imaginary other's fingers coming away slick with grease and sweat when they finished.

"Do you wanna use my tub, Dad?" I asked during dinner, both of us shoveling grilled cheese sandwiches—with burnt tops—into our mouths, cold tomato soup dripping off the blackened crumbs.

"Nuh," he said. Distracted. Like a much more important debate raged inside his head. I wondered if he noticed any waves or thrashing as I had. Or like what I'd heard inside of Mom.

*Mom.*

I stopped mentioning her to Dad after the first couple of days. The last time, he'd laughed in my face. No pleasant, "we're sharing a joke" laugh either. Something mean and spiteful in how he did it. I ran from the living room, my bare feet against the carpeted hallway. The floor outside my parents' bathroom was damp to the touch. Not wet, not soaked, or anything so extreme. But damp enough so I noticed when a sudden jolt traveled up from the soles of my feet. I stopped in front of the bathroom door.

It hung open a crack. Like the first time. This time I squeezed my eyes closed. Refusing to look. I held my hand over my ears too, trying hard not to hear. I didn't want to find Mom with her skin whiter, paler, all wrinkled from head to toe. I didn't want to hear her humming, moaning, kicking red, decrepit water onto the tile floor.

Thrashing. Like something held her down. Pulling on her, pulling her under waves of her own making.

I backed away, one step, then another. Until I was able to turn from the door and run to my room. It marked the last time we said anything about her.

Until one particular dinner. Then, Dad stood from the table, and held his right hand out palm first, giving me a command. *Stay.* "I'm gonna check if your mother wants to join us."

Of course, I'd finished my soup and sandwich and stored Dad's in Tupperware containers in the fridge, long before any sign of Dad's—or Mom's—presence reached me. When I passed him in the hallway on the way back to my bed, I caught Dad leaning against their bathroom door, his forehead close to the jamb.

"C'mon, babe. Please come out. C'mon, please. Let's talk about this. Let's talk about what happened. What's happening..."

I got set to sneak past him. I'd put on my PJs and practice reading from the chapter book I checked out from the school library. But then the bathroom door opened.

Mom stood there, not wrinkled or pale as I'd expected. Her skin still retained the silver sheen, but it'd gone so smooth I saw the blood vessels underneath it. They glowed red, full of life. Her hair appeared in blinding white flashes, longer and wind-swept like some romance novel heroine, painted with bold brush strokes. She'd tied an emerald silken bathrobe around her. But it was far too small to contain everything she'd become. Her full breasts and fuller belly strained against the confines of silk. She wriggled her swollen toes on the hallway carpet.

Her eyes were solid black like she'd stepped wet and ravenous from a nightmare. Eyes black like one of those deep-sea trenches where no light reaches and strange creatures thrive in the shadows. These fully-dilated pupils swept over me, and Mom's nose wrinkled. She grinned with lips closed and every single tooth pressing against skin. Then, she turned away from me—her son, moving as though she'd judged me and found me unworthy of attention.

Later, I'd wonder if she detected meatier prey.

*Blood in the water.*

Dad reached for her, his arms outstretched like some lumbering beast. He encircled her in an embrace. Pulled her against his five o'clock shadow, undershirt, and sweatpants. She radiated against the dullness of him, a black-light gleam against mundanity.

He patted her back. His whisper near her ear came as a choked cry. "I forgive you," he said.

His hand wandered over his love, seeking the part in her gown and access to her swollen belly, sloshing with seawater weight as she shifted her feet.

The house grew heavy with the scent of saltwater, warm sands, and fish guts. I pulled the neck of my t-shirt around my mouth and nose, trying to block out the more noxious elements. But the scent reminded me of drowning in a swirling cloud of beach rot.

Mom took Dad's hand. "Hey…"

She cut him off before he finished. Pulled the hand up from its brief contact with whatever swam inside her belly, whatever pressed its angular face against the taut skin of her stomach. A pointed nose and sharp rows of teeth showed through her belly the way *her* teeth were revealed behind *her* closed lips.

The bile rose through my insides, a rushing swirl of sick. I couldn't watch anymore, so I ran on nervous tip-toes, covering the brief distance to my room, my bathroom. I turned back once and found Mom still holding Dad's hand tight. She brought it to her lips. The thin pale strands of flesh parted.

I couldn't tell from where I stood, but it looked as though her teeth grew sharper and were stained red as well.

Mom must've sensed my eyes on her. She turned, head snapping toward me so fast her eyes on me stung like a sunburn. "What's the matter, dear?" she asked, her voice sounding as though she spoke from underwater. "You look green in the gills."

I avoided watching what happened next. I fled into my bathroom, vomiting up tomato soup. Red and chunky. Like afterbirth. My child of sickness to be flushed away and forgotten. After I finished, I wiped the back of my hand across my lips, mashing flecks of red into the skin.

I couldn't make myself turn on the water in the sink, couldn't wash my hands and face, or scrub away the remnants from my lips, teeth, and tongue. The idea of water, even the cool, clear water from the tap, touching my body, repulsed me. Instead, I curled up against the cabinet under my sink and rocked myself back and forth, until I reached some state closer to sleep than not.

***

After some time, the sound of water rushing through the pipes woke me. The tile was cold and, at first, I mistook the chill for the wetness of water. I assumed it'd found me, despite my best efforts. I sprang to my feet and nearly cracked my skull against the countertop edge. When it didn't happen, both hands held tight to the marble finish. The spigot sat dry, unused. Nothing from my bathtub either.

Of course, I knew the source of the rushing waters all along. Their siren's song emanated from the hallway. The lights were on in my parent's bathroom. I moved toward the center of the house, walking the hallway the way I'd come before, swimming upstream against safety and security. The door to their bathroom gaped open. The cold and hot water taps for the bath were turned to their fullest settings,. For a moment, I watched water hammering water. The heavy spray from the spigot struck the overflowing surface like a whalemen's spear stabbed into some nineteenth-century leviathan.

The blood-red waves crested over the rim of the tub, spilling liquid onto the floor and rising past the exterior. I leaned into the bathroom from the dryland of the hallway, uncertain why the waters remained confined to the bathroom and showed no signs of spilling out to me, either to coat my toes or wash me away.

Both options remained within the realm of possibility.

From the hallway, I searched the rising red waters of the bathroom, looking for dark shapes under the surface. My breath emerged in hitched gasps, expectation squeezing my insides. I believed I'd find Mom and Dad both, floating under the crimson wastewaters.

Instead, I encountered nothing more than the gentle slap of water against their bathroom vanity and the clawfoot tub from which it'd originated.

The sound produced a hypnotic effect. It continued with no sign of ceasing, the rhythmic shushing and slapping repeated ad infinitum. If not for Mom's moans reverberating through the walls, I'd have stayed there forever. When I heard her call from the bedroom, I felt as though she'd reached out to me through the ether, ensnaring me with a new spell.

The way she'd grabbed Dad.

I stumbled away from the bathroom, exhausted. Like I'd swum to the middle of the ocean, stroke after stroke, legs kicking...until I stopped. I'd taken myself somewhere past the crashing waves. I'd entered a place of isolation and calm, where my companion was the eternal dread of knowledge—knowing I shared space with beings who'd called these waters their home, long before man was a dream on the planet. It took years before I put words to this experience. And even now, they're insufficient.

When you're young, everything else's ancient. It's hard to appreciate time in its rawest form.

Mom and Dad were naked. Nothing I hadn't seen before, though I'd reached an age where they fled from my eyes, as though the sight would turn me to stone. Where my mother's body remained shimmering and beautiful in its exaggerated proportions, Dad's appeared as a droopy, sad, and commonplace thing. In this exposed form, he became a nervous swimmer approaching the ocean in plastic inflatable floaties. The splotchy whiteness of his skin reflected against her vibrant radiance to resemble zinc smeared across a sunburnt nose.

She lay on her back, shoulders propped by a mountain of decorative pillows. Her legs parted, her sex revealed. It looked as though a scouring occurred, a savaging of her vagina. From an angry red algal bloom like a warning to all who approach, pink tendrils slithered out. My father's cock was a plumped blister in comparison, a veiny crustacean stripped of its protective armor and crowned with steel wool silver hairs. Any notions of eroticism in this tableau fell by the wayside.

Something between fear and ecstasy crossed my father's face. He stumbled forward on his knees, a lowing like some lost cow separated from the herd accompanying his movements. Soon, he'd reached his partner. In his moment of penetration, I heard his words to her. "I forgive you."

Her eyes opened black again. Twin abysses in which my father stared and found something staring back at him. Twice over. I watched him try to stop, try to pull back and deny her.

"We don't need your forgiveness," she whispered.

Her legs spasmed, shaking. The lips of her sex appeared as coral reef embellishments, ancient living, life-giving structures, straining under the emergence of the creature who'd swum inside her womb since she'd left us for the ocean. The beast grew until there was no more room inside of my mother and its exit was preceded by another wave of blood. It sprayed gouts of chunky red fluid all over Dad. The shark inside Mom's belly chewed its way down and out of her, thrashing its sleek silver body, scraping fins along her musculature, and gnashing its many rows of needle-sharp teeth.

Then, it found the bait my father dropped from between his legs, ramrod straight and heavy with more blood. Dad stiffened at the sight of sudden death. Frozen until the shark inside Mom's belly opened its Jack-O'Lantern grin wide enough to feed. It pushed, swimming out of her, straight ahead, and onto the bed. It grew as more and more of its storm cloud silver form appeared and fins slapped the stained sheets.

Soon, the shark—the new life placed inside Mom by someone, *something* else—had devoured my father's manhood. But then, the creature kept going, kept eating, until Dad broke inside this monster's jaws. Burst like a swollen grape.

And opposite, my mother withered away with a smile on her lips. Like a mermaid's purse burst open into a desiccated black husk.

Leaving me alone.

***

But not alone.

The realization hit me as I tip-toed into the bedroom and encountered the shark's eyes, black like his father's, staring at me from the soiled sheets and flaccid innards of my parents. *Our* parents. Well, our mother at least. My half-brother's mouth opened and closed, unable to articulate, out of his element.

"There you are," I said. He thrashed among the bloody remnants of my father, following me with his black eyes. The gasping red of his mouth went faster, faster. Leaving me with a decision, another life on the line in my family tree.

Except there was no decision to make, no true conflict. I placed a plastic tub in an old wagon. I filled the tub with water and salted it after. And then I whispered a prayer and pushed my brother off my parent's bed, into his new home.

I left the house, pulling the wagon behind me. No one except me and my brother—the shark from our mother's belly. I headed for the ocean. Deciding I'd help him find his father, return him to life under the waves.

A sudden mewling cry, rippling the surface of the water, drew my attention. I looked into the clear water, to where the shark swam. Under the flippers, a tiny arm with a tinier hand and tinier fingers emerged. Reaching for me. He wrapped his extra digits around my thumb and we set off in search of shelter, love, and food.

# Your Selkie Lover

You wait on the rocks one last time, with the cold and damp soaking through the windbreaker you picked up at the hotel gift shop. The salt spray from crashing waves is all too familiar now. Still, you breathe in deep, hoping to pick out a trace of her scent, some early sign of her approach. You repeat the familiar question over and over in your mind, *Will she come back this time?*

***

But your heart already knows the answer, whether the rest of you is ready to accept it or not. It's gone the same way every morning since your sunrise-tinted descent from the pier following the first night of your vacation—when Jeff didn't wait for you to come to bed and instead rolled over to face the wall, clad in his stained crew-neck t-shirt and fraying gray boxer shorts. Snoring with an intensity to match the hotel's box fan in the window. You slammed the room door when you left, but you know he didn't move a muscle. The certainty lingered deep in your bones.

Once you struck the water, the current took you, or so you believed. Knocked unconscious from the impact of your body, covered in that thin, silken nightgown, against the harder-than-it-looked surface, but awoken by saltwater in your nose and mouth, filling your lungs when you turned the wrong way, you floated along. *Merrily, merrily.* You thought maybe it was true, maybe life *was* but a dream. You moved through the water with a purpose divine, until reaching the rocks. The same rocks where you're standing now—nearly one week later.

On the first morning, something nudged you harder than lapping waves and forced you to scramble up the rocks. Slick, oily fur brushed your exposed backside. It tickled. So, you laughed. The adrenaline rush of leaving the cold water to enter even cooler air took hold and your laughter transformed into a howl.

There you were on the rocks, shivering. Crying. You couldn't tell if the tears came because you were happy to survive or because you were sad for the same reason. Finally, you wiped the salt-stung sides of your hands beneath your lower lids and took in your surroundings.

Seaweed dredged up from the water decorated the rocks like verdant fondant. Under the risen sun, every stone shimmered, enhancing the magical aura of this strange outcropping. Down at the water's edge, you observed the still, silent presence of a brown and lumpy misshapen thing. A boneless mass of smooth auburn hairs.

Setting aside the weariness of your muscles and bones, setting aside the chills wracking your body with additional teeth-grinding pain, you stood on loose legs. You held a hand out, stretched toward the pile of fur low on the rocks, waiting where land and water mingled.

Then, she made her presence known. Appearing behind you, like she was with you all along.

Her hand rested on your shoulder, providing a light touch still firm enough to stop you. You turned your head and found her there. Where the water turned your baby-blue nightgown transparent revealing every fold, every wrinkle, every pocket of fat hanging from your arms, and the sweat stains below your breasts, the perfection of *her* nakedness stood in sharp contrast. That was your initial assessment, of course.

Looking back, you understand how much you ignored in this first encounter. The blue tint of sunlight on her skin, the pink flesh-like residue falling from her with every confident stride across the rocks. The way her teeth appeared sharp in her smile. How the odor of fresh fish wafted from her breath as she introduced herself.

Except, it wasn't an introduction, was it? She never gave you a name and she never asked for yours. She settled in beside you, keeping some space between. "This is my favorite place to watch the sunrise," she said.

You watched her instead of the sun. And she returned your gaze with the whole of her being. Your heart exploded against your chest, raging against the confines of your bones. Mostly metaphorically, but your cool skin still tightened. Your nipples stiffened against the damp fabric. To relieve the tension, both physical and emotional, you shared your story with her. Letting it spill in torrents. Feeling as though you needed to say something to explain how you got on those rocks but never questioning why she was there, appearing the way she did. You shared every moment that brought you to the end of the boardwalk pier. You omitted the details between your fall and her revelation on the rocks. Because you didn't understand them—not yet at least.

She listened, her eyes wider than the sun revealing burnt umber shading in the parting clouds. Never interrupting. Never looking away. When you finished and the tears came, she smiled.

But it wasn't a mocking smile, so you welcomed its appearance. You sighed and let your pain blow away from between pale, blue-tinted lips. Your eyelids closed and she used the moment to lean in closer.

Her tongue was sharp and rougher than expected. She licked your tears. Up and down, erasing them from your face. Brushing the top of her tongue over your eyes. You'd opened them at her initial touch. When you opened your mouth—*to do what? protest? balk?*—her tongue slipped inside. Her taste was seaweed and sashimi. Plants and raw fish, an animalistic hunger taking hold. This encounter wasn't *love*, this was *nature*. Your hands grasped her shoulders, prepared to pull her body into yours.

But she pushed away.

"It's getting late," she said, brushing past you as she sashayed to the rocks. Heading for the water and the brown and gray fur at the water's edge. Her hip rubbed your ear as she passed. You turned your head too late to savor the cool vibrancy of her skin.

"Too late?"

You repeated her words like an echo.

She turned back to you, still unashamed of her nudity. A long, slender finger pointed to the sun. "More people will come. They'll see."

In your heart, the sinking feeling spread. You thought you understood what she meant. You remembered childhood crushes, study breaks in college with peppermint mocha-scented kisses stolen behind the stacks, followed by flushed skin and awkward goodbyes. How would you explain if other people caught the two of you? What explanation could you offer Jeff so his response wouldn't make you feel like shit?

You nodded. Thinking you both spoke to similar concerns.

She lifted the fur and draped it across her body. Not pausing to wring out the water from the hide. Instead, she let the heft of the water-logged fur pull her down. Her knees buckled. Her hands reached behind to pull the hood...no, the head, an animal's head...over her own.

Even then, you didn't stand. Whatever held you in place, whether magic or the everyday sensation of feeling overwhelmed by the world around you, was strong enough to keep you grounded. Everything was too much, the same way everything was always too much. You sat and watched. The sun blinked. A new impossible thing. Spots formed in your field of vision. You shook your head, white clumps of hair striking your forehead like graduation mortar tassels.

The seal watched you from the rocks. Not long enough to establish a concrete connection. But enough to leave you with vague intimations of the truth.

Then, she slipped off the rocks and into the water, diving deep where you couldn't follow her descent.

She was gone.

And you realized the emotion twisting up your insides was approaching love after all. Coming closer than anything you'd experienced in recent memory. And maybe even longer.

You hurried back to the hotel, ignoring gawking passersby. Ignoring Jeff's questions, you shut yourself in the bathroom. You stood under the hot water until you suspected your skin might melt off your bones. When you finished, you wrapped yourself in the towels provided by the housekeeping staff. The chocolate brown cloth sapped the water and steam from your skin. Until you believed you'd drawn out the memory of what you'd done in the pre-dawn hour, how you'd survived and found something new, something worth living for.

***

You sit at the water's edge this last time. Your sandals rest beside you. A robe stolen from the hotel bathroom waits on the other side, carefully folded. Your feet dangle in the water, and you trace circles with your toes. Until something breaks the surface, the cold saltwater bristling of her snout touching the underside of your foot. In the days previous, you waited patiently, removing yourself from the edge so she'd have time to remove her sealskin and dress in the robe you provided. But this time, you don't want to wait. You get on your knees, so close you could fall in the water all over again. Though at least it'd make for a shorter trip this time. Your hands are outstretched, reaching into the water to touch her in her *other* form.

You're practicing what you'll say when she's out of the water, free of the fur. "I don't care what you look like when you wear the sealskin. If I want you, then let me want *all* of you."

If she's eavesdropped on you while surfacing, her response isn't an indignant one. There's no trace of the frustration woven into every syllable Jeff's muttered in your direction, with his lidded eyes and a drunkard's slur before dinner's even served. She slaps a flipper up, breaking the surface and sending tingling droplets into your eyes and mouth. You teeter for a moment. But right yourself in time.

You slide back from the water, chastised but not embarrassed. Corrected, but not shamed. When you've cleared the gritty ocean water from your eyes, streaking it across your cheeks like tears and you've wiped your finger under your nose to collect the sea-salt remnants of snot, by then she's slipped onto the rocks and changed.

It still surprises you how fast she executes the transformation. It takes a moment before you remember, *she's magic. She spends most of her days as an animal.*

*But then again, doesn't everyone?*

She keeps her distance, considering you with her eyes but remaining still otherwise.

***

Not like the other times. Those other times, she took your hand and you ran, laughing, screaming. The two of you found a secluded cove with smooth sand untouched by shells, seaweed, or other detritus. Under the shade, you laid her down on fine-grained white sands and tasted her. Then, you'd let yourself be consumed, be filled. Her fingers parting her sex and yours. With a greedy look in her eyes and an insistence paired with her teeth biting your lip, she refused to let you go when you tried to pull away from her kisses. The message was clear: *No, we CAN have it all.*

The second time you made love on the beach, when your sweat-dappled legs shivered and she pulled you up to your feet and pointed to the sun, you hobbled back to the rocks together. Limbs tingled with a pleasurable ache. Some college boys with soft cheeks and hangover-puffy eyelids gawked at the pair of you. You played the devil, licking your lips, and winking before you pulled on your clothes.

It did the trick, serving as enough of a distraction for *her* to put the sealskin back on and return to the water.

Your heart beat in double-time all the way home. The bravery that fit so well before shrank smaller and smaller with each step. The boys followed, keeping their distance. But their words grew louder and louder. Until you snapped like a twig in a windstorm when the hotel room door closed behind you.

Jeff was there. His hands by his sides. When you came closer, he opened his arms and embraced you. He sniffed your hair. Breathing in beach air, saltwater on your fingertips, her sweat and yours mingled. After you sobbed against his shoulder, he pulled back and told you to go take a shower. No reproach in his voice. No anger, no sadness. Nothing more than a cold, clinical assessment.

If you're honest, it hurt worse than any slap, punch, or choking, he could've given. You stared at him through tear-misted eyes, finding in his indifference the future of those boys who'd followed you "home." How many of them would wake up to missing wives and a vague sense of an inevitable ending?

***

"Do you have to go?" she asks. She sows the seeds of doubt with soft kisses along your clavicle.

This time, you're the one who pushes *her* away. Even with the distance created, your selkie lover reaches her human hands under your blouse. Her palms are wet and cold against your breasts. Your nipples stiffen in response. You let your arousal speak for you—the way it's gone this entire week previous. Allowing lust and desire to dictate the terms of your interactions. Setting aside Jeff and the broken relationship this vacation was supposed to heal, you turn the question back on her and ask, "Do you have to stay?"

The wind off the water picks up speed and intensity, so you shout the final part. As if to show your willingness to meet her halfway, you peel off your blouse. The swirling winds take the fabric as if it never belonged to you. It spins above your heads, like an artist mixing paint on a palette. You don't reach for it. You let it go.

Once it's gone, you return your attention to her face. Her mouth's open, but her tongue's still. Her lips recede in a pantomime frown. The sob issuing from deep inside isn't human, but an animal's howl of pain. You imagine her in the sealskin, trapped in a fisherman's net. Panicking, choking. She makes a raw and bestial sound. You hesitate from comforting her with words or deeds. It's hard to believe your arms around her will still the ache she's expressing.

***

It's confusing; all those days, when you had each other, you'd assumed you were the one trapped. Stuck in patterns impossible to break. She never told you much about her condition. "This is who I am and *that* is who I am," she said, running her hand along the backside of her fur. You tried to touch it, but she stilled your hand.

"Please don't," she said.

***

Now, she gulps down sob-choked breaths. When she's finished, you're ready to let her fall into *your* arms. You're ready to offer comfort. Not the way she did, a stranger sensing a connection and wanting to help.

Not like Jeff, offering a pittance in exchange for...nothing more than keeping things the way they are.

You give her a lover's comfort, the raw reassurance that you'll find a way to make her stay, to keep her with you. And you recognize the contradiction inherent in those two statements. And you don't care, do you?

Someone coughs. Or they laugh. It's a sharp cruel thing, so when you turn around you expect to find those college boys returned. Haven't you expected they'd come back, egging each other on, elbowing each other, and getting bolder with their fantasies? Bold and black, dark impulses reflected in an infinite pool of the void.

But there's no mob of slavering ghouls, ready to feast on your happiness and these moments of pleasure. There's Jeff.

Whatever cruelty you heard from him is gone by the time you've taken in his presence. Vows disappear like the fading smoke of abandoned fires on the beach. His blank expression speaks volumes. The connection was lost long before you forgot the words you swore to each other.

"So, this is where you've gone all these mornings," he says.

She pulls on your arm, trying to move in front of you. As though her silver-blue skin's shield enough to keep you safe.

But you won't let her. This time, you'll stand before her. You'll be the one to keep her safe. You won't drop your chin, won't lower your eyes, or mumble words of apology. You won't wait until you've returned to the hotel and fall to your knees, begging forgiveness for your indiscretions.

Not this time.

He comes closer. Closer. You note the way he breathes through his mouth, snorting and snuffling like a truffle-hunting hog. You catch the burst blood vessels across both eyes. Like he's brushed his teeth with gin. A couple of shots of courage. Then, a couple more.

Then, seven more for good measure. *Right, darling?*

He stretches out, reaching for you. You and your lover move as one like you're dancing before him. But not *for* him. This waltz is for the two of you alone.

He falls, feet slipping on the slick rocks. He tumbles down, groaning. Wet skin slapping on wet stone. You look away, deep into the dark eyes of your lover and watch what happens in the reflection.

Your husband falls, sliding down the rocks, and when he stops, there's the sealskin. His back hitches as ragged breaths come from his ragged form.

Think about it, when did he ever make it out of the hotel? He's pale, like some creature dwelling in the dirt and dark. More likely to show up under a rock than in your heart or dreams.

You don't have to tell her, and she doesn't have to tell you.

You both know.

The sealskin's smooth to the touch. You stroke the fur and find her fingers coming from the opposite side. Until you clasp your hands and pick up the skin together. It's a tighter fit on Jeff than on her. You pull and stretch it. Flippers cover bloodied knuckles. The head's bloated, its seal eyes bulging. Giving the creature a clownish look. A dumb dull animal's moan issuing from jagged teeth.

Your feet push against the creature's belly. Her feet join yours. Working in tandem, until the splash. Bubbles rise to the water's surface. Then, the seal's head breaks through as well. The beast tilts its fattened head at you, confused. Perhaps there's a flash of recognition there?

The seal barks, a loud note, like a drunkard blurting out obscenities.

Your lover pulls you close and swallows your laughter with a kiss. Then, another and another.

She's so good. Sometimes you wonder what it'd be like to wear her, to witness the world from her dark eyes.

And sometimes, you wonder if she ever feels the same about you.

# The Middle Sister's New Situation

U ntil she looked up and noticed the bright halogen lights shining onto her bed, Cassie never knew her bedroom lacked a ceiling. She considered all the times before when she'd laid on top of her covers, staring up at nothing at all, thinking about the future. Or more likely thinking about why everyone always paid so much attention to her big sister Mara or her little sister Jordyn. Cassie was certain there'd been a ceiling above her in those moments. There were plenty of times when her Dad or Mom stood in the doorway or sat on the edge of her bed, telling her they loved her. She was sure a parent or an uncle, her sassy Grandma Gladys or her sharp-tongued Grandma Ruby, or even Phyllis Dorkel the neighbor girl who snuck into their house at night to watch everyone sleeping, would've said something about the lack of a ceiling in her bedroom. It wasn't right; living, sleeping, and doing her homework, in a room with no ceiling.

Though, in fairness, Cassie wasn't even certain there *was* no ceiling over her bedroom. She figured, if there was one, it existed above the row of lights, the circular halogens bolted in place across a burnished gun-metal gray strip. It was far too bright for her to make out anything past that point after all.

However, in moments of personal crisis, she always knew what to do. She reached a hand up, putting her fist against the wall behind the headboard, and rapped her knuckles against it. Her sister Mara's bedroom sat beside hers with both beds set so they were head-to-head, separated by the wall.

But when Cassie knocked, the sound her fist produced wasn't the bass drum echo she'd expected. Instead, it made a thin, empty sound, as though she'd tapped against a bird's hollow bones. Hollow bones were the part of a bird's anatomy allowing it to fly. Human bones, filled with blood and meat, stuff called marrow, didn't lend themselves to flying.

Cassie assumed she'd learned that particular anatomy lesson in school the day before. But with the unrelenting light shining on her, her confidence in her memories drained away. She took in every detail surrounding her: The teddy bear family nestled at the foot of the bed. The bouquet on her dresser, there since the day her Mom died. Its petals always white and unwilted.

She pulled her feet free from her princess-bed comforter. Her cotton nightgown was white with a yellow smiley face in the center, displayed across her chest. "At least one of us is smiling," she whispered.

Then, she waited. Like she expected something to happen. Like someone would "ooh" or "ahh." Laugh or applaud.

Instead, silence. Her heart beat through the thin material of her nightshirt. But nothing else made a sound.

"Mara?" Cassie's question was soft, probing. Even with the illumination above her bed, the girl sat up and shivered as though she'd awakened inside a cool, impenetrable darkness.

The darkness gave nothing in return.

She tried again. Louder. "Mara?"

Finally, she got a response. Someone cleared their throat and spoke with a voice flecked by cigarette ash and boredom. "Security! Stay where you are!"

Cassie's bed grew warmer. The sheets turned wet beneath her. It smelled like a bathroom.

Or at least it smelled like what Cassie *thought* a bathroom smelled like.

She couldn't recall the last time she'd used one though. It wasn't something she viewed as strange until she woke up and found out her bedroom had no ceiling and the walls of her home were hollow like the bones of birds. She found herself thinking about many things she'd never put much thought into before once those things happened.

A man stood in her doorway. Khakis hitched up past his waist and a black dress shirt paired with a silver patch hooked over the front pocket. "Something-Something Studios," it read. Cassie found it hard to concentrate on the words. It was harder still for her to gaze past the beam of light emerging from this stranger's flashlight.

She sat back in her bed, her upper body pressed against the headboard. She waited for the man to say something. There was always something for someone to say whenever they stood in her doorway. Some clever, yet confused aside.

But the strange man in his ill-fitting uniform swung the light around, imprisoning Cassie between the beams, and kept up his silence.

A small, sharp noise escaped from between the girl's lips. A squeak, like a mouse caught by its foot in a trap.

She wished for hollow bones like the birds, something she'd use to spread her arms and fly away.

"What'd you say?"

Squinting in the light, Cassie looked across at the waiting man. "What?"

"You said something about birds?"

The girl swallowed, wishing her big sister would come save her. Mara made everything better. Or if she didn't, then at least she drew the spotlight away. Cassie believed if her sister was there, then the possibility she could sneak away, unnoticed and unremarked upon, would arrive.

But her sister remained absent.

The man stepped closer. Cassie pulled the covers over her body. Cocooning herself in cloth. "Where am I?" she asked. "What's wrong with my room?"

The light lowered. "Ms. Van Essen?" the man asked.

The new silence made Cassie uncomfortable and set her to itching more than the sheets against her bare skin had. But she willed herself to reply.

"That's not my name."

***

"Would you get the damn flashlight out of my face? And outta the young lady's face while you're at it?" The studio medic's eyes shot daggers across Cassie's bedroom, hitting the security guard dead on.

The uniformed man flicked off his flashlight and muttered something about "trespassing."

But Cassie didn't understand how she could trespass. After all, she was in *her* bedroom. Which was supposed to be in *her* house. But for whatever reason, it wasn't.

She didn't understand how her room ended up on what they called a "studio backlot." It wasn't something that matched with her life experiences in the slightest. She was a small-town girl from a small-town family whose members sometimes had misunderstandings and went on adventures but always learned a valuable lesson in the end. *At the end of what?*

She struggled to find the lesson in this particular instance.

A small, but growing, part of her suspected she was experiencing some strange dream. Except this dream didn't follow the rules of her usual night-time fantasies. The security guard looked nothing like her father. The medic bore no resemblance to the boy she liked who sat across from her in Social Studies. In most dreams, Cassie recast friends and family in any new or esoteric roles. As though her subconscious didn't see the point in expanding her repertory company beyond those select few.

On the other hand, Cassie was relieved to *not* find nosy neighbor Dorkel sticking her nose into her dream business, watching her through an open window.

However, relief faded fast when she looked past the guard in the doorway—the one that *didn't* lead to the upstairs hallway of her home the way it was supposed to. Behind the man, practically peering over his shoulder, Phyllis Dorkel's face loomed larger than in life. "Phyllis..." The name was all Cassie got out.

The medic turned, uncertain who or what Cassie was referring to. Trying to make it clearer for him, she pointed a trembling finger at the unmoving, unwavering Phyllis. She noted other shadows, human head-shaped shadows but larger, like giants, surrounding the super-sized grinning visage of her neighbor. Cassie recognized magnified versions of Mom, Dad, Mara, and Jordyn.

*But I'm in here. Not out there. I'm still small.*

The medic pushed past the guard, entering the place beyond the bedroom. He returned to Cassie's bedside, carrying her family and Phyllis. Except it wasn't them. It was a cardboard cut-out, blown up past life-size. He set it in front of the girl. "Ms. Van Essen. Do you remember this show?"

He pointed to words printed below the eternal smiling faces of everyone Cassie cared for. *Plus Phyllis Dorkel.* "OUR FAM, NEW SEASON, SAME SMILES."

The words seemed so generic, so empty of meaning, Cassie shook her head when reading them over and over again. "My name's not Van Essen. It's Clark. It says so right there."

In smaller letters than the epigraph she'd contemplated, the words "The Clarks, Wednesdays at 8/7 Central" read as another enigmatic riddle. "What happens Wednesdays at 8?" Cassie asked.

The medic smirked. Behind him, the security guard held his phone out, pushing his thumb across the screen, lost in a new task. Still, he found time to snicker at Cassie's question. She stood with arms crossed over her smiley-face-covered night shirt, sticking her bottom lip out and mumbling, "Oh, c'mon!"

"Like on the show..." the security guard said, not looking up from whatever held his attention on his phone screen.

Cassie didn't care if the security guard was someone in charge, she didn't care if the medic was helping. She didn't care if she'd woken up in a dream or crossed over into somewhere else entirely. She launched herself forward, her right hand balled into a fist. She imagined what Mom or Dad would say, how they'd offer quiet, soothing words about how violence was wrong and how she should talk it out, ask questions until she got the answers she needed.

Except she'd tried and got no answers. Her room wasn't real and her parents were nothing more than cardboard standees. She decided the old ways of problem-solving were due for a massive reassessment.

But before she reached the guard and connected her bony knuckles with the folds of pink sunburnt flesh above his collar, the medic grabbed her. His hand squeezed around her wrist, tighter than she'd expected. Everything was *more* in this new world. The lights, the sounds, and now the touch of another. Something between suspicion and nagging doubt gripped the girl, leaving her wondering if every memory she had was a dream and if this strange, aggravating experience was her first genuine taste of reality.

She wished she didn't feel like such an outsider in this alternate version of her bedroom.

"It's when your show airs," the medic said, finally providing an answer. He let her go, having stopped her progress and her would-be attack on the guard.

"Show? What show?"

"The Clarks. The television program you used to star on…"

"No, it's not a show. Or a program or whatever. That's my family. What's going on here? Why's my room here? Why do you have a picture of my family and Phyllis? Is this another one of her schemes? Is this a…what is this?"

The words she wanted sat on the tip of her tongue, but something stopped her from speaking them. Images too depraved and horrifying for a teenage girl to contemplate appeared at the periphery of her mind's eye. Just out of reach.

"Jesus, sweetheart. Whatever dope they got you on sure did a number on ya, huh?"

That was the security guard. His thick eyebrows furrowed in equal parts annoyance and something a bit more sinister, more vindictive.

He moved closer, filling the space between him and the girl in moments. Cassie wanted to run. She considered hiding behind the medic again, letting him serve as her human shield. But a tension hung above her interactions with that stranger as well. So, she planted her feet between the two men and waited.

The guard held out his phone, displaying the screen for Cassie. A grainy internet video was queued up. Cassie leaned forward to read the title. As she did, the medic's hissed disgust, sounding as though he'd transformed into a nest of snakes into which the security guard had thrown a match. "Don't show her that!"

But it was too late.

The guard's pudgy index finger touched the "play" button on the video titled "JORDANNA 'CASSIE CLARK' VAN ESSEN AS YOU'VE NEVER SEEN HER BEFORE."

Cassie watched. In the video, she saw *herself*, but it was not herself. Not any version of herself she recognized. This other, wearing too much make-up, hair slicked back against the top of her head, smiled for the camera, like she was born for it. No awkward shyness of a middle sister here.

Cassie stared, as her other spoke in a hazy, dream-like manner to a gruff-voiced man operating the camera. Wherever they were, this other Cassie ("Jordana" as the camera operator continued to call her) oozed sensuality and...sexuality, traits Cassie had no experience with or reference for. The dark of the midnight bedroom on the tiny phone screen was the type that'd send Cassie scrambling next door to Mara's room, where they'd hide under the covers and giggle until morning. But the other Cassie was a fungus or vampire bat, a being thriving in the darkness. The night-vision function on the camera made her eyes glow like a hyena in a nature documentary, stalking its prey. Preparing to feast.

Cassie wanted to look away. She *needed* to look away. But watching herself engaged in acts of carnality made for too compelling an image to turn away from. Again, it took the medic speaking up for anything to happen. "Put that shit away, man," he said.

The security guard laughed, a cruel braying chuckle, before stuffing the phone into his trouser pocket. Except, he conveniently *forgot* to turn the video off, and the low moans of the other Cassie and her paramour echoed from the confines of the laughing man's pants.

***

In Cassie's dream, everyone kept laughing. She walked down the stairs, which spilled out onto a scene of chaos in the living room. Mara was trying to get bubblegum out of baby sister Jordyn's hair. But she'd only managed to get her own tresses stuck as well. Their strands commingled, a tangled mess of princess blonde and serious black connected with a bubblegum adhesive. "Cassie, thank goodness you're here! Come help us get this gum out before Mom and Dad come home."

Something beyond instinct, something like the pull of gravity itself, compelled Cassie toward her sisters. She was all set to say something half clever like "What's gumming up the works, ladies?"

She saw down the path to its inevitable ending: She'd get stuck too. Then, she'd say, "Oh c'mon!" And everyone would laugh once again.

*Or maybe Jordyn will say what she's always saying: "Noooo never!" And they'll laugh at her. Maybe Mara will roll her eyes, siphoning off the last of the laughs.*

*But what about Cassie?*

Regardless of the result, the siren's song of fate dragged Cassie toward the sticky conclusion. However, she stopped short of her siblings when she noticed half of their living room, hell, half of their house was missing.

Like someone had taken an industrial saw from rooftop to floor and lopped off part of the Clark House like some gangrenous limb.

Men and women in t-shirts and jeans, pencil skirts, and expensive suits alike, milled around the nebulous space where the Clarks' living room should've continued but instead ended like an abandoned art project. These others, with paler skin, thinner lips, and duller hair pointed cameras and huge oval-shaped black microphones at Cassie and her sisters. They watched them, waiting for what Cassie would do and say next.

Cassie looked to the side. A young woman in tortoise-shell glasses flipped through a stack of printer paper with words printed on the pages.

"Jordana, your line's..."

Cassie opened her mouth. Something like her voice followed. But these were not her words. "I know what my fucking line is, bitch."

She slapped both hands across her mouth. They came up so fast and so hard, the impact stung her teeth.

For their part, Mara and Jordyn turned their heads, joined by gum into a ridiculous two-headed monstrosity, and offered nothing more than a blank, unconcerned look to their middle sister. All Cassie wanted to do was return a reassuring, soothing expression of her own. Something to let them know she was okay. Making her way through a minor identity crisis, but okay nonetheless.

Except when she looked closer, she noted the pins where hair and make-up stuck the wigs onto the heads of Tina (or was it the other twin Lena) and Jennifer. *No, it's Jordyn and Mara. They're my sisters. They've got gum stuck in their hair and soon I will too. Because this...*

*...has happened before.*

***

The woman in the black suit sat on the other side of the long desk whose mirrored surface was too dented and pockmarked to hold a true reflection. She paused the video playback on her laptop. She'd turned the screen so Cassie, sitting at the other end of the long silvered rectangle, could watch.

Cassie resisted the urge to say "Oh, c'mon."

She'd learned a lot over the previous days, starting when she woke in a world that wasn't hers. The main thing she'd come to appreciate was the value of silence. It wasn't something she was used to. Every memory was filled with either a rapid-fire back-and-forth exchange of one-liners, the laughter or melancholic sighs of strangers, or a constant upbeat soundtrack of Top 40 hit knock-offs. And even when the noise went away, when Cassie looked deeper into her memories, she was met by an undercurrent of blaring static.

But out here, in this place everyone—from the hospital to the police station to this other *special* hospital she now found herself in—called "the real world," they let things stay quiet. Cassie suspected it was because no one ever knew what they'd say until they were forced to say it. Fighting for words and trying to pull out the correct response from an endless combination was exhausting. She'd never had this problem before.

The woman in black spoke first. "So, Jordana, do you see in the video? Do you understand?"

The way the woman looked at her, eyes large in their sockets, made Cassie sure she needed to answer. So, she tried. "I see it. But I don't understand, ma'am. This happened to me. I know it did. But not like that. I never...I wouldn't talk that way."

The woman in black arched an eyebrow. As far as Cassie was concerned, it was a far better reaction than the typical scoffs, wide-eyed stares, and muffled laughs behind clenched fists she'd been subjected to previously. Even worse, the lewd gestures made behind her back that weren't hidden fast enough when she turned around. An arched eyebrow was different. It showed something closer to interest.

Cassie elected to keep going.

"My sisters Mara and Jordyn got bubblegum stuck in their hair..."

"When was this?"

Cassie resisted the urge to say "Wednesday at 8." She knew it was correct for one world, but not for hers. "I don't remember, I..."

"Say the first thing that comes to mind."

Like the woman knew what Cassie was thinking and was trying to catch her out. The girl opted to say the second thing that occurred to her. "The fall. The season changed..."

"What happened after you walked downstairs and found your sisters in the living room? What'd you do next?"

"I...I...I went and..."

The woman in black—a doctor, a therapist, a secret agent (Cassie couldn't say for certain and she hadn't asked)—let the silence work in her favor. With her nerves heightened, Cassie looked at the tabletop. Her reflection was a patchwork quilt, a pock-marked monster mask. One eye comically enlarged, made her appear as a cartoon version of herself. Those intense eyes and accompanying lashes resembled some baby-doll vamp incarnation of Cassie...Jordana...whoever she was supposed to be.

Staring into her too-large eyes, Cassie followed the path of tears down her face, slipping and sliding between this cracked, imperfect skin. She wanted to reach down and pull this other version of herself inside her mouth. Either devouring it, destroying it, or hiding it away.

But she knew she couldn't.

"I don't remember!" Cassie screamed the words and there was nothing cute or sassy in her delivery. Those three words made her throat ache and her head throb. The tears weren't a few clear lines of wetness on her cheeks, they were a mess of damp, salty water, off-white in coloration. Staining her. Marking her.

She wasn't sure she'd stop with the floodgates opened. She worried her tears would fill up the room like she was Alice lost in Wonderland. But the woman in black stretched an arm across the table and gripped Cassie's hand. A squeeze, tight but not restrictive, pulled the girl back to reality. Or whatever version of it she'd found herself in.

"I understand," the woman said.

Then, after another moment passed where Cassie wiped tears and snot away with proffered tissues, the woman continued. "This tape's from the aborted Season 3 premiere of *The Clarks*. Filming was halted following an incident—several incidents—with the young woman who played middle sister Cassie Clark on the program for seasons 1 and 2. The actress was Jordana Van Essen. Following what the studio deemed a violation of the ethics clause in Ms. Van Essen's contract her character was written off the show for the third season. Rather than recast, the producers elected to never acknowledge the existence of a middle sister on the show. The Clarks are now a two-child family for viewers around the world."

Cassie had heard the words before. Or some variation of them. Even when repeated all those times, they still made no sense. She'd seen this *Jordana*, her depraved bad-girl doppelganger, worse than any *bad person* she'd envisioned from her old life.

Even while she was interrogated in other bare, empty rooms like the one she found herself in, others pulled up videos of her counterpart, trying to break her. They wanted her to admit that she and this "Jordana" were the same. However, live videos made it clear—*they were not*.

"I'm not that...woman," she said. "I'm a teenage girl."

The woman in black stared back, her expression indicating: *I wasn't finished yet.*

She continued. "The medical testing we've performed shows you have the body of a twenty-one-year-old woman. The same age as Jordana Van Essen. (Though she often played younger.) DNA records suggest you *are* Jordana. Matching her to the chromosomal level. And yet..."

Her fingers clicked and clacked across keys, pressing them with expert precision. She brought up a website, the name on the search bar reading "CELEBRITIES EXXXPOSED." There was a blurry version of this other Cassie, looking like the one glimpsed in the tabletop reflection. Her other lay topless on a beach, sunburnt, with round black shades over her eyes, making her look like an ebony-eyed demon.

"Ms. Van Essen was photographed by paparazzi in Cancun while sunbathing earlier today. You've been here in our facility all day. Those conclusions speak for themselves."

Cassie nodded.

"And yet..."

"And yet." The woman in black closed the laptop.

"Do you watch television, Cassie?"

Cassie squirmed in the hardbacked chair she'd sat in for the session. She wasn't sure how to answer the question. But she forced herself to try. "I've watched TV. I know I have, but..."

"Do you remember any specific shows? Any episodes? Any moments from those episodes?" The woman in black spoke over Cassie. Her delivery was more intense than before.

"I watch shows. I watch..."

Cassie trailed off, looking to the side. The white-painted door of the bare-walled room showed one window, a tiny peephole the girl couldn't look through when seated. She wished she could. She wanted to find what waited beyond the white walls and the black clothing of the woman sitting across from her. Tears filled her eyes once more, blurring the white and the black. Until they turned grey, wavering like the static she heard in her head.

The woman in black's fist came down hard on the tabletop, jolting Cassie from her attempted mental retreat. "Cassandra Clark, look at me."

Cassie listened and looked. She remembered once when her Mom called her Cassandra. It might've been the earliest memory she had—strange since she was at least thirteen when it happened. *I told her, "Oh, c'mon, call me Cassie, Mom." Everyone laughed. It felt good. Even though I missed out on everyone laughing...*

"Have you ever heard of a television show called *Strange Reports*?" asked the woman in black.

Cassie shook her head.

"It's an hour-long dramatic series, a bit of a science-fiction/monster-hunting vibe to it. An idealistic rookie agent teamed with a jaded, cynical veteran...working to contain unexplained phenomena leaking into the 'real world.' Huge hit and tons of people love it. They've even got conventions dedicated to it. The thing setting the series apart when it was first announced was the casting of a woman as the gruff vet. Dressed her all in black, made her mysterious. You could tell she cared, but also might scare the crap out of you."

Cassie nodded.

"You've never watched an episode of *Strange Reports*?"

"No...no ma'am. But what does this..."

The woman in black turned the laptop back around to type on the keyboard. Cassie waited as fingers tapped at the keys. When the woman returned the screen for her perusal, Cassie studied the image on display. She saw two handsome, jawbone-perfect male actors. One with shaggy blonde hair and baby-blue eyes. The other a black man with a trim white goatee and a grimace on his face. Beneath the duo, the text read "STRANGE REPORTS, PREMIERING SOON."

"Where's the woman?" Cassie asked.

"They re-cast the part after the original pilot was filmed. Some network executives got the sense the dynamic was a bit too close to *The X-Files...*"

Cassie returned a blank expression, having no idea what the woman in black was talking about. The woman waved it off and pressed forward. "...never mind. Plenty of time to catch you up on the classics later. The point is, instead of a woman, they went with an older, black character actor. The show was still a hit. The actress who was originally cast as the veteran investigator moved on to film. She's a huge star now. Won an Oscar last year. The kind of big-time celebrity you'd never think would *slum* it in television."

The site the woman in black pulled up featured a photo slideshow. The image of the two lead actors from "Strange Reports" marked the beginning of the presentation. More images slid past, stills from the series, behind-the-scenes images, and red-carpet premiere photos from the "Strange Reports" movie.

And there she was, glamorous in the manner of a living goddess, wearing a gorgeous dress like a second skin. Everything about her was made to look larger than life. The movie star who was meant to co-lead on "Strange Reports." The woman who *was* on "Strange Reports," until she wasn't.

But if you took away the dress, the blown-out hair, and smoky eye make-up, then dressed the star in all-black...

"It's you," Cassie whispered.

The woman in black shook her head. "No. Not really. She's played me. We share the same appearance. But I'm me. I come from a world written into existence by two men from UCLA. But when the time came, they sacrificed my world and remade it to one where I wasn't needed. So, I ended up here...in theirs."

"Like me?" Cassie asked.

The woman in black stood up abruptly. Her worn heels thumped against the floor as she crossed the room. She placed her hand under the girl's chin, tilting it up. "Look at me," she said, "There's *no one* like you. You understand?"

Cassie hesitated but then nodded.

The woman in black offered her hand, pulling Cassie up so they stood on equal footing. "Let's say my 'character' made me a bit more open-minded to what'd happened and helped me understand what I was to the people of this reality. But as the 'gruff, cynical' veteran, I guess I was also wary enough to keep a low profile, make something for myself in this world..."

Cassie thought about her bedroom. She thought about her sister waiting on the other side of the wall. A wave of anger, deeper than she ever remembered experiencing, passed through her. She balled her hands into fists again. The woman in black must've sensed this frustration heading toward a boiling point. Her arms unfurled like long, creeping vines. Going for a hug, but awkward in her execution.

Cassie noticed and couldn't help but chuckle. Even with tears in her eyes, it was good to laugh. She reached behind her, taking the woman's hands in her own, bringing them down to complete the embrace. "There you are," she said.

She pressed the side of her face against the woman's black dress shirt, leaving salty tear stains behind. But smiling. The woman in black choked out an answer. "They called me Marie Esteria. I kept it. You can keep yours too. But only if you want..."

Cassie nodded.

"I understand," she said, "Or I'll try to...I don't know what to do."

The woman in black, Marie, took the girl's hand in her own. "You'll get used to the feeling. Trust me, it's the best. The uncertainty of everything."

That evening, in the facility run by Marie Esteria, Cassie settled into a bed similar to her old one, princess sheets and all. One of the assistants, a cute boy with the dirty blonde hair of a teen heartthrob hanging over his eye (the main character in a teen drama edited out of existence when the actor playing him OD'ed) asked if she wanted the cardboard cut-out of her family—the one she'd encountered at the studio.

"No, thanks," Cassie said.

"Cool," the dreamboat said. He had a smile Cassie would consider later, no doubt about it.

Once she clicked the bedside lamp off, Cassie lay in darkness. Not fading away. The silence was her companion. No music. No applause. Just a lost girl going to sleep. She reached back and knocked on the wall above her headboard.

She lay back against her pillow, waiting for her sister to respond.

# Rat Suit King

Derrick took his lunch break in Bryant Park, eating a bodega ham sandwich on a bench he shared with an old-school type of businessman who wore a crisp gray suit and a disapproving perma-glare. The man in the gray suit pulled his legs close together, striving for as much separation from Derrick as possible.

While Derrick was also dressed for work and was also dressed in gray, the similarities ended there. On Derrick, the pajama-soft shag of the lower half of his mascot costume bulged over his all-black tennis shoes. The costumers sewed extra padding around the crotch of the outfit's lower half, which connected to similar padding placed inside the suit's upper portion. A long, pink tail sewed from felt scraps extended like some Muppet's penis from Derrick's padded backside, then dangled between the bench slats.

On further consideration, Derrick understood the true source of the businessman's disgust likely came from the cloth-and-foam rat's head, gray-furred with red mesh eyes, a black nose, and a yellow-toothed "smile" which had covered his face until he brought his take-out back to the bench. It was an ugly visage, all angular and gnarled. Derrick ran a nervous hand over his head, freeing sweat-plastered hair from where it'd almost cemented itself to the top of his skull. The businessman wrinkled his nose and swung his legs around so he sat at an uncomfortable diagonal, nibbling at a rye bread sandwich with nervous squirrel-like energy.

Perhaps Mr. Businessman smelled Derrick's sweat and morning breath wafting from inside his rat mask. The younger man reached down, his hand wriggling to find purchase in the space between the musky interior of his costume bottoms and the slick, sweat-soaked gym shorts he wore after learning about the prevalence of fungal infections among his fellow street mascots. "Costume crotch" they called it, and one experience with it was more than enough for Derrick. His fingers closed around a tin of Altoids, which he worked up into the light like he'd become some claw machine made flesh.

He smiled, relief whistling between clenched teeth once the tin emerged from his sweaty depths. He popped it open and downed three tablets. The mints carried a slight chemical odor, but he chalked it up to their less than sanitary storage conditions. His mouth pursed as the mints did their work. He moved to make eye contact with the businessman, hoping to exchange a look saying, *Is this better?*

But the businessman was gone, rushing away to finish his lunch elsewhere. He power-walked down the winding sidewalk, eyes forward and shoulders sharp.

And rushing in the opposite direction, *toward* Derrick, another older man approached, wearing an expression also conveying immense displeasure with the lunching man in the rat costume. Derrick groaned, understanding that no amount of Altoids would solve the problem moving closer and closer.

"Hey, you! Hey, Derrick!"

The approaching man wasn't a dwarf, but close enough. He looked as though he'd be inconvenienced by a shrubbery at least. His skin was wrinkled, like laundry taken fresh from the washer and draped over the man's bones without a trip to the dryer first.

The top of the small man's head was crowned with shoe-polish black hair (and its odor up-close made Derrick more than a little suspicious Chen used *actual* shoe polish for dying purposes). He wore a sleeveless undershirt and khaki pants held up with brown leather suspenders. He kept up his reprimanding chorus. "Derrick! Hey, boy, I'm talkin' to you!"

Spittle flew from the angry man's mouth as he came closer. With the precious time he knew was left, Derrick shoveled in a few more bites of salad, swallowing a hefty chunk of Crouton, before grabbing the mask and placing it over his head. "I know, Mr. Chen, I know!" He held his hands up, palms out. Tiny and pink inside the voluminous sleeves of his rat suit.

The Crouton and salad dressing went down the wrong tube. Derrick coughed—a wet, breadcrumb-caked sound fading into a belch. "Shit," he muttered, coming to grips with the fact he'd be stuck with the scent of stale salad burps swirling around his face for the remainder of his shift.

Which happened to be the rest of the day.

As it turned out, off-the-books, mascot-costumed panhandlers didn't get eight-hour days or even lunch hours. They got whatever the hell Mr. Chen wanted to give them. Especially if they wanted enough of a cut to barely afford rent and keep the lights on. (And sometimes Derrick had to deal with not having lights on or with washing his clothes in Starbucks bathroom sinks.)

"What's rule number one?" Mr. Chen asked, arms folded across a sunken chest that devoured the cloth of his t-shirt.

"Make people happy?"

Derrick knew it wasn't the answer Chen sought, but he couldn't resist having fun with the man, his "boss," "handler," "pimp," or whatever he wanted to be called.

Chen took the bait. "No! No! No!" He shook his head and made X's with his arms to indicate *how* wrong he believed Derrick was.

"You dressed like a rat. No one likes rats in New York City. People see rats, they say 'Ewww! Rat! Go away, rat!' They see *you*, they think the same thing. Except rat, a real rat, will just run away. Squeak-squeak, have a nice day. But you—you ask for money so you go away."

When he finished, Chen cocked an eyebrow toward Derrick, as if to say *Have I made myself clear?*

Derrick nodded. He was grateful that Chen missed his eyes rolling inside the costume head.

The older man picked up his admonishments where he'd left off. "Rule number one for always and forever: keep your costume on. No one sees you. No one knows you. They see rat. Only *rat*."

Derick stood, the round shadow of his inflated costumed body and the shabby circles of his ears, covering Mr. Chen in a black embrace. Every movement Derrick made felt stiff and exaggerated, the consequence of moving the bulky fabric around his lean and lanky body. "I'm sorry, Mr. Chen. I really am."

Mr. Chen shook his head once again, but this time lowered his arms from his chest. Despite the yelling and exploitative hours he inflicted on his employees, Derrick liked the man. After all, Chen took a chance on him when he believed the city was set to chew him up and spit him out. After the acting gigs he'd come to town expecting to land post-college never materialized and even temping gigs dried up and withered away before he got enough time for the office admins to remember his name,

Derrick found himself teetering on the edge of becoming a cautionary tale.

"Hey! Hey! Hey! Quit dreaming. Okay?" Chen snapped his fingers by the enlarged rat ears of Derrick's costume.

Derrick looked at his boss, the pink rat nose tilting upward until it nearly struck Chen's chin. The old man leaped back, surprisingly spry for his age—which fell somewhere between Derrick's dad's age and ancient, as far as the costume-wearer could tell. "Watch out," Chen muttered like he'd avoided a leper's touch or some worse fate.

Derrick dropped to his knees, ready to focus and get back to work. The clear plastic bucket with "TIPS" written in Sharpie on the side waited for him, with a pile of dirty bills and some tourists' pity spare change representing all of Derrick's earnings for the day. On the ground, with his rat-tail-decorated ass poking out from under the bench, he felt more ridiculous than ever. But as he pulled the bucket closer, the sight waiting for him proved more shocking than anything he'd witnessed in the few years he'd spent in NYC.

Peeking out from under the abandoned orange grease-stained cellophane that once held another dime-a-dozen "authentic" New York pizza slice, an *actual* New York City sewer rat's tail swished and swiped across cracked cement and leaf particles. The wormy appendage with its gnawed-on pink flesh grazed Derrick's knuckle. Quick as he could, Derrick drew his hand back to the gray fur of his costume, exhaling with a feverish hiss. Like a violently deflated beach ball. At the same time, instinct kicked in and he raised his head for a quick exit.

Too bad he hadn't moved far enough away for the necessary clearance. The top of his head struck a copper screw, oxidized green by weather and time. He moved so fast he felt the cold metal splitting through the fabric on the foam rat head, driven down to break the skin at the top of his actual head.

A warm trickle of blood from his scalp followed.

Before he could register the injury, Derrick became preoccupied with what happened before his eyes. Because when the stained mozzarella-encrusted cellophane fell away, Derrick found himself confronted by, not one large black-furred, pink-faced rat with yellowed teeth hardened by time in the garbage cans and subway tunnels of Manhattan and the other boroughs, but a swarming storm cloud of the befouled rodents, four, five, ten, twenty. More. The hideous creatures writhed as one, undulating under splattered grease, making it near impossible for Derrick to get an accurate count.

He watched the rats, tangled by their tails, through the black mesh eyes of his mask. He ignored the wet sensation at the back of his blood-slicked head until the wooziness threatened to overtake him. Their shit-stained tails interlocked into an elaborate knot-tying puzzle. Like if he reached in and grabbed the right tail he'd pull them all apart. He studied the vermin, hypnotized by their synchronized motion. Rather than crawl straight ahead or back and pull the mass in multiple directions at once, the rolling blob of rat flesh moved in a circle, rotating and spinning as one unit—like the Earth around the sun.

Until a triptych of rat heads stopped near Derrick's other hand, the one he'd left on the ground for balance when he'd pulled its partner close to him for safety. Like some murine Cerberus, the black-eyed rats opened their mouths and sunk teeth into the flesh of his exposed fingers. He pulled his entire body back, eyes watering so many actual tears fell down his cheeks. The scent of saltwater musk filled the costume.

"Motherfuck! Jesus!"

Mr. Chen's arms crossed again when Derrick straightened, wincing. Chen tapped his foot against the cement. As if to say, *Well, time's wasting...*

Derrick pointed to the horde of rats hiding underneath the bench. Not considering how strange he must've appeared—a grown man in a rat costume used for panhandling, gesturing with violent fervor at some muck-encrusted rodent circle that had attacked him.

"Rats! Rats! They're all...stuck together, like a...like a..."

Except he lacked the words for what he'd witnessed.

"Yeah, yeah, okay, okay. Whatever you gotta do to get in character, boy," Mr. Chen said, waving a hand and dismissing the urgency Derrick was trying to convey.

No one else in their vicinity moved in response or even acted like they noticed, outside a few hipsters and teens playing hooky, snapping pictures of the odd rat man. Their pictures might end up trending on social media for a few hours at best. Then, they'd disappear, leaving nothing more than a memory. Internet ephemera.

A low throbbing pain spread up Derrick's arm. He'd freed himself of the rats, but they'd done a number on him all the same. One took the skin off his fingertip, the other ground the wrinkled skin from a knuckle, and the third serrated the cuticle around a fingernail.

Thinking of the immediate pain and his desire to make someone understand, Derrick reached for Mr. Chen and pulled him to the bench. "Look!"

With his bloodied hand, he'd grabbed the old man by his suspenders. He pointed with a clean hand. But when Derrick peered through the slats, all he saw was the greasy cellophane pressed flat to the ground.

Then Mr. Chen's hand rested on the chest of his rat suit, pushing Derrick back with intense power. "Hey! You're bleeding, you know?"

Fat drops of scarlet fell from the scrapes, scratches, and bite marks on Derrick's hand. Some of the blood splattered on the ground. Some of it hit the bench. Some landed on Mr. Chen's bare mummified shoulders. And some was smeared across the grey fur of Derrick's rat costume.

To Derrick's surprise, Mr. Chen's next words weren't a reprimand. Even though the sharp-angled wrinkles on his face suggested a man with vengeance on his mind, he instead pointed to Derrick's wounded hand and said, "You need to go to a hospital, okay?"

Derrick shook his head, moving his rat snout back and forth. He didn't have the money for a trip to the emergency room or the patience for a free clinic. Plus, he figured he'd need as much money from his rat suit panhandling as he could manage.

Not that any of it was reaching him anytime soon. He wondered how much it'd cost to get his rat costume back to a state Mr. Chen would find acceptable.

"I'm fine," he said, before puking inside the rat head.

Mr. Chen put his hand over his eyes and turned away, leaving his employee to the remnants of his lunch dribbling into the body portion of his costume. "You owe me either a clean costume or a new one. Okay?"

*Okay.*

***

"Four hundred fucking dollars!" Derrick's voice cracked as he bemoaned the cost of a replacement costume, alone in his apartment. Everything he'd found online from Amazon to eBay suggested a three-figure investment was required if he hoped to attain a replica of the rat mascot costume used by Mr. Chen in his menagerie of panhandling larger-than-life characters.

Of the costumed panhandlers he stationed across the city, Chen worked with children's TV show monsters, superheroes, and a bunny—who was or wasn't an Easter Bunny depending on the time of the year. Derrick was his only rat. As a result, he wore Mr. Chen's only rat costume.

Sitting at the found-on-a-street-corner-probably-has-bedbugs tiny table in his kitchen, Derrick flipped over the stained costume's head to take another look at the musty interior. The insides stank of Lysol from the bathroom and some potpourri shavings he'd stolen from an unmanned counter at Macy's. Derrick hoped the brown chunks would work like sawdust in elementary school classrooms whenever a kid hurled and the janitor didn't want to invest too much time or effort in cleaning.

This time, Derrick played both kid and clean-up man. His fingers were marred by dried blood turned black and yellowed blisters he prayed weren't signs of infection. Mindful of the tenderness of his injuries, he brushed aside the matted fur poking through the inside of the mascot's head until he found the tag once more.

"REX RATTUS 1 OF ?"

Derrick pulled his hand back like he'd touched a livewire. He brought his injured fingers to his chapped lips.

He had no clue what "REX RATTUS 1 OF ?" meant. He didn't know if it referred to a company or a costume type or what. "Rattus" meant something about rats, he figured.

Frustration taking a firm hold, Derrick banged his other hand against the tabletop, hitting the birdshit-splattered wood so hard his broke-down laptop launched upward and then landed on its side. The next thing he knew, some warm and wet substance dribbled down his chin.

He quickly realized that he'd nibbled open the wounds on his hand and was bleeding anew onto his costume. Making it that much harder to clean.

"Awww shit."

Though it wasn't like any cleaner he'd tried, via phone calls *or* abrupt in-store appearances, had showed any willingness to accept the assignment. The in-person visits resulted in wrinkled noses, evil eye stares, and one zealous Hispanic woman repeating a litany of *Ave Marias*, while pushing Derrick out the door of her shop. Phone calls weren't much better, though they lacked the added sting of having someone else witness embarrassment reddening his gaunt cheeks.

As a result, buying a replacement suit—despite Derrick having nowhere close to the necessary funds—presented itself as the most viable of his impossible options.

*In other words, he was well and truly screwed.*

***

Add to the mix, the pounding headache Derrick endured all day, kicked off by a rude awakening from his roommates as they rose, showered, and departed for their 9 to 5's, making thinking hard in general.

It wasn't that his roommates were loud or obnoxious. Far from it, if anything. Derrick trended more to black sheep than the rest. Keith, Lamont, and Trix were all nose-to-the-grindstone, keep your head down and do the work-kind of New Yorkers. With their publishing, tech start-up, and finance jobs, the trio existed as the epitome of the dream Derrick had brought to the big city. They'd managed not to stumble out of the starting gate though.

That morning, after Derrick saw the tangle of rats and stained his costume, his roommates' normally subdued routines sounded like a subway train screeching to a halt on silver tracks, sparks striking old bricks and cement, exploding his dreams into a million fragments. He hid under the stiff under-washed covers on his cot (the one bed that fit in the converted closet space serving as his bedroom), awaiting their departure.

The back of his head aching, he exited the room nose first, sniffling. Staring at his bedraggled reflection in the gunmetal-grey surface of the fridge, Derrick discovered he'd kept the rat costume on all evening. When he took the mask off, his hair sat plastered on his head stuck in place by sweat and dried sick. He was certain he'd reached his lowest moment. Not just since moving to New York. But of all time.

***

"Seeking SPECIAL Mascot Costume: RATTUS REX?"

Derrick's eyes glazed over as he reviewed the post he'd composed for Craigslist. He'd managed to upload some photos of the rat costume propped up against the far wall of his bedroom. Lucky for him, he'd snuck a peek at a scrap of paper on his roommates' desk with the wi-fi password on it. (Apartment consensus at the time was that Derrick shouldn't have access until he switched to paying his share of the rent with cash and not IOUs.)

He listed his posting under special requests. The way Derrick saw it, someone would have to be *special*—as in the touched in the head variety—to own another costume like the strange, creepy rat one Mr. Chen loaned him.

Speaking of the devil, as soon as Derrick's finger pressed the Return key confirming he wanted to post the ad, his old cellphone, a blocky and cracked monstrosity rattled against the tabletop. *Caller ID: CHEN.*

Derrick leaned back in his chair, considering the light emanating from the screen as though he'd recovered the Holy Grail. He pulled the phone close, pressing it tight to the side of his face. "Hello?"

"Hey, boy, you working today or what?"

"But I don't have...it's not my day. I worked..."

A long pause followed from the other end of the line as Derrick flailed, scrambling to bring up the calendar on his laptop. His heart dropped to his stomach when he read the date in his toolbar. Not just one day had passed since the rat costume debacle, but two. Remembering to exhale, his breath whistled through his teeth and traveled through the phone line to Mr. Chen.

*"Yeah, you're late. You got my costume cleaned yet, too?"*

The words sounded clear as a bell in Derrick's head, so it made no sense when Chen cleared his throat and spoke those same words again. "Yeah, you're late. You got my costume cleaned yet, too?"

"Yes, sir. I—you didn't give me a chance to answer before."

"What the hell're you talking about, boy? I didn't say nothing to you until now."

Derrick found himself struck by the overwhelming urge to drop to the floor, imagining Mr. Chen standing in the back of some noisy market, on the phone with his wayward employee. In this vision, Chen stood in Derrick's path.

He pictured the raised cuffs of the old man's khakis raised above the ankle, showing enough skin for Derrick to turn his head and take a bite. Teeth piercing flesh, saliva mingling with fast pooling blood.

"You okay?"

Mr. Chen's query interrupted Derrick's reverie. A translucent sheen of drool decorated the young man's chin. He wanted to end the call. *Needed* to end the call. He intended to say something short, simple, and to the point. "I understand, sir. I'll be out soon. And as for the costume, I'm working on finding a replacement. Don't worry, I'll spare no expense."

But what came out of Derrick was a series of gut-rumbling grunts and high-pitched squeals. He hit "End Call" fast as possible. Threw the phone across the room where it bounced off the closed makeshift plywood door.

Like it had a life of its own, the beat-to-shit phone leaped into the opening where the rat costume head connected to the rat costume body. Swallowed by the darkness, the phone screen's ambient light was absorbed and further thinned by its new confinement.

Derrick leaned forward, fingers stretching to their limit. Before making contact, the sickly green phone screen lit up in full. Buzzing vibrations shook the costume, causing the hollowed-out rat to shift, appearing ready to hop off the wall and crawl on its own. Derrick's hand closed around the phone and he pulled it to his face.

Someone was calling him. But he didn't recognize the number.

Before he answered, another call interrupted the previous one.

Then another. And another. On and on...

Derrick sat on the laundry-strewn floor, cross-legged watching the calls come in. Sometimes a text message blipped across the screen. The initial trickle of communication morphed into a deluge of confirming messages. Derrick was mistaken, plenty of people owned an extra rat suit.

When he worked up the nerve to check his messages, each one said the same thing. "I have RATTUS REX 2 OF ?," "...3 OF ?," "...4 OF ?"

One after the other, counting up with no end in sight. Derrick stopped counting when he got to "19 of ?" There wasn't much point in going further.

Strange enough that he'd placed his classified ad five minutes previous.

He also had to contend with the fact he hadn't included his phone number in the listing.

***

Derrick stepped out from the subway entrance at Union Square, eyeing buskers and other non-costumed panhandlers. His rat suit still smelled terrible. He couldn't for the life of him remember why he'd opted to wear the stained and damaged costume instead of carrying it with him. Maybe in an oversized garbage bag—some fitting luggage for the hideous outfit. Of course, he also wasn't sure why he'd brought it in the first place.

*To compare it to the others*, he told himself with a feigned confidence he hoped would quell his raging nerves—despite all evidence to the contrary.

At least his roommates would be happy with the suit gone. When he'd emerged from his room near the end of the day, they were waiting, standing outside the door in a semi-circle of judgment with their heads bowed. Derrick stood with the rat's head tucked under his arm. Not to be intimidated by the prejudices of his roommates, he walked the gauntlet, showing each one the tag. "What's this mean?" he asked each of them.

They were smart. Capable too. Certainly more so than Derrick the failure. Keith and Lamont both wrinkled their noses, sneering at Derrick as though he'd come up to them shit-faced drunk with puke all over the front of his shirt. (Which wasn't too far from the truth.) Trix appeared set to react the same, but they stopped themselves. They read the words of the tag with an eyebrow raised. "Rattus Rex?" they asked.

Derrick nodded, as the matted fur of the costume's neckline tickled the space between his chin and Adam's apple.

"It's Latin. Means *Rat King*."

With that said, Trix lowered their eyes and ducked away from the semi-circle of judgment, miming like they were busy with some minor dishes-related matter in the kitchen.

Derrick returned this silence in kind, hoping his uncertainty showed through clear enough. Trix coughed, breaking the thick, roiling tension between the roommates. Then, they said, "You know like when a bunch of rats get their tails all tangled. It's an urban legend though. People say they become like one many-headed creature. Working as one. Total bullshit though."

*I saw one.*

When no one answered, Derrick tried again.

*I SAW ONE.*

His three roommates locked eyes with him, their lips stayed closed but Derrick heard them inside his head. Speaking as one.

*Please leave.*

So, he did. Because he wanted to prove them wrong. He wanted to prove *everyone* wrong. His parents. His teachers. The acting coaches who'd overpromised and under-delivered. His roommates. Mr. Chen.

***

Derrick hadn't told Mr. Chen to come, but his boss showed up regardless. His shirt was still stained from Derrick's two-day-old vomit. The sight made the young man wonder how badly Chen needed the percentage he took from all his panhandlers.

As the sun set behind the massive towering buildings of Manhattan, blacking out swaths of cement and asphalt, the old man tottered forward on unsteady legs. Limping as though his ankle were bitten, like Derrick daydreamed.

"Shit." Derrick hoped he'd remembered in time, hoped he'd sighted his elderly boss before the old man caught him. He pulled the rat's head over his face, inhaling caked-in puke, sweat, and the salt of his tears. But at least he wore the right visage for the job. At least he wouldn't get yelled at.

He waved his tiny pink hands. Staring across the closing gap between them on the brick walkway, he hoped Chen would approve. But when the old man caught sight of his wayward employee, Derrick looked past him. In the span of seconds, something else had caught the young man's eye.

Viewed through the black of the rat head, Derrick saw another person wearing a Rattus Rex costume, waving *their* tiny pink hands. They emerged from behind a bush or a tree, it was hard to say. One moment,

Mr. Chen limped forward, cheeks sucking in and out with each labored breath and pained step, then another rat appeared.

Derrick lowered his hand. He positioned it near the neck of his costume, prepared to discard the bulky headpiece once more. After all, shouldn't he want to meet the costume-seller face to face? Human face to human face. But he stopped himself. A voice spoke in his head. *"Don't."*

It was his voice, the inner monologue playing inside his head at all times. Same as anyone else might experience. But it was *more*. Like there was an echo in his skull, bouncing off the insides. A distant chorus, as though marchers were heading down Fifth Avenue to the Park. Almost chanting his inner monologue in harmony.

Almost.

When Mr. Chen moved close enough to take in Derrick and his soiled rat costume, he stopped short. Derrick watched the interloping rat coming up behind his boss. He expected the costumed stranger wouldn't stop in time. He'd pictured the rat costume's bulky mid-section colliding with the old man.

But the second rat proved nimbler than expected, coming to a halt short of contact. A heavy wind blew between the concrete and steel buildings surrounding the Park, then dipped lower to wriggle through the surrounding trees.

As a result, Derrick couldn't hear much over the whistling and shrieks. He settled for trying to lip-read Chen's trembling mouth and follow the pantomime hand and head gestures of the other rat. It appeared as though this second rat spoke first. In response, Mr. Chen turned his head, eyes widening when he came face to snout with the other costume-wearer. When he returned to gaze at Derrick, Chen appeared confused, like he'd been hit on the head.

Derrick glanced lower and saw the man's too-thick socks stuffed into his shoes, already turning salmon.

*I should do something. I should say something.*

He stepped forward, moving to join the fear-frozen Mr. Chen and the new rat. But when he took his first step, the impact sent psychic ripples through concrete and brick, passing over Chen and linking Derrick to his new rat companion. He saw an Asian man, not as young as Derrick, not as old as Chen. A narrow-cheeked, quiet, unassuming figure, compelled by some force he couldn't explain to leave a promising career in government back in the home country to travel a dangerous path to America. Finding himself unwanted by all. Not looking for a fight, but always ending up in one. Black eyes and blood-crusted nostrils. The need to feel something, to connect in some way. But afraid to show his bruised and battered face.

Then, he found the rat costume. When he wore it, the other man never asked for anything. He didn't want donations of money or food or booze, no offers of shelter either. He'd refuse them all with a curt shake of his rat's head He wanted to wear the costume and be near people. That's all he wanted

At the same time, as Derrick experienced all of this, the young man felt his life, his story traveling out to the other man. An exchange of ideas, of states of being.

"Derrick?"

Mr. Chen's question came as an afterthought, barely noticed by the two men in their costumes.

"More?"

This time, the pair of men in rat costumes heeded the old man's query. As Derrick stood opposite his counterpart, they both turned their foam- and felt-covered heads, watching more costume-wearers emerge. Some wore the costume loose, others cinched it so tight one could make out the outlines of belly buttons and beer guts. When the others came close enough, Derrick stumbled on the cracked concrete.

A flood of faces and stories washed over him.

An African American kid from the Marcy Projects, trading in candy bars and subway dance shows for the Rattus Rex.

A college student from Bard, her hair in dreadlocks and skin the color of the year's first snowfall. Black eye-liner, black lips, and a choker. She wore the costume for her clients.

Some faces, like Derrick's, were variations on a theme.

They formed a circle around Mr. Chen. His stained shoes and sweat-soaked sleeveless tee were close to glowing amid the sea of gray. His mumbling, panicked breaths provided a backing track.

Inside his head, Derrick enjoyed twenty, thirty, fifty conversations all at once. Each one understood and clear.

Something scraped against the back of a nearby bench. Derrick's head turned and his rat face moved with him. Whiskers again scraped against other whiskers.

The last arrival emerged. Derrick beamed under his costume.

The businessman, the one who'd turned away in disgust, that afternoon when Derrick first glimpsed the rat king.

*Except maybe it wasn't disgust showing on the man's face. Maybe those lines etched on his brow and around his harsh, thin lips had come from jealousy.*

Regardless of past intention, Derrick waved the man closer.

Their circle was complete.

Mr. Chen was on the ground, pushing against their gray-covered legs. Trying to carve a path out. But Derrick knew he wouldn't succeed.

Working as one already, the assembled rat costume wearers turned their backs to each other. Their faces were all the same on the outside after all. So what'd it matter if they saw each other? Derrick shuddered inside his suit, and the low moans and gasping squeaks of his fellow rats told him the others were experiencing something similar. The long pink tail that hung loose behind bench slats slithered and writhed against his backside.

It stiffened, poking out straight, again reminding Derrick of some abominable erection. Then, it sprung out, pulling him backward. The tail of the costume wearer behind him did the same until the two met in the middle.

Wrapped around and around and around each other. Then another tail came from a diagonal. And another from the side. Another and another. When they connected, the faces Derrick observed faded from memory. As though, they were becoming one more indistinguishable part of his being.

One after the other. Connecting to Derrick and giving themselves away. Until the last tail, the one belonging to the businessman, all clean and pristine. Probably straight out of a plastic costume bag shipped to the man at God only knew what cost.

When they linked and the man's face faded from memory, Derrick flexed. Ripples sent out like shockwaves, moved the other costume-wearers. Those nameless, faceless, story-less parts of the Rat Suit King.

Through the mesh eyes of not just his *suit*, but all the others, Derrick observed the world. It was New York City after all. The world in microcosm. A world long ago given to the rats even if the humans stuck around, persistent in not getting the message.

Derrick's eyes bled a creamy, chunky red like tomato sauce, leaking through the mesh of the rats' eyes. Soon, there was no Derrick. No distinction between that being's head and all the others. There was only the Rat Suit King.

***

The Rat Suit King found the old man crawling across the waste of a knocked-over garbage can. Moving in a pinwheel pattern, arms outstretched and yellowed teeth gnawing through the fabric, the Rat Suit King fell upon the man like a buzzsaw. Biting, gnashing, clawing.

Consuming flesh and drinking blood, whiskers awash in gore. Scraps of clothing, broken bones secreted away for building its nest.

When the feasting finished, the Rat Suit King and all its covered bodies, tails, and heads, fled into the shadows. As filling as the old man was, a morsel pulled apart and savored, the Rat Suit King needed the darkness to lick its wounds, to let gangrenous rot set in, and to let its legend grow.

Across the park, faces bobbing like drunken fireflies. Someone bearing witness to a transformation. Ten, twenty, fifty visages becoming one. A murmured chorus set to spread across the boroughs.

*All hail the Rat Suit King!*

*All hail!*

# THE BIG GOOD BOY

The "Big Good Boy"—the Kaiju-sized canine serving as the latest incarnation of simulated apocalyptic disaster for Faiz and the rest of the Norbrid Disaster Preparedness Team—slept across the remains of downtown San Francisco. The creature's breaths came in low-pitched, rumbling growls. His thick auburn tail twitched. Every thump against concrete, steel, and asphalt, sent debris clouds swirling into the smog-draped sky. Buildings left standing wobbled and swayed like drunkards at the exit after Last Call.

Luckily for the NDPT, the creature's slumber gave them a small window in which to execute their plan. But even then, they couldn't be certain how small a window they were working with.

Katya placed Faiz at the back for their sweep of the area. With nothing but destruction and the backsides of his teammates in front of him, Faiz didn't envy Katya her position as leader, way up there at the front of the line.

The NDPT covered each ruined quadrant with methodical efficiency, as Katya had drilled into their souls. Like the others, Faiz kept his service weapon drawn, but his finger off the trigger. He'd be damned if Katya would get the chance to drag him when the mission wrapped, for something as basic as "mishandling equipment."

"We're doing rescue work, not dropping bodies," she'd always say.

The rest of the team crossed the ruins of a once-bustling intersection. The former heart of the city had turned into a metallic jungle, overrun with broken and still-smoking remnants of cars, buses, and God only knew what else under the rubble-strewn surface. Those clouds of man-made poisons floated across the sky like herds of elephants. The team moved between the gaps in the expelled fumes, the flashes of sickly blue showing the way forward.

Faiz stopped short, left behind on what was once the other side of the street.

The foamy, yellowish liquid—drool from the mouth of the Big Good Boy—dribbled down a crooked traffic pole light. The foul dollop landed a foot behind Ramon. If Faiz had kept pace, he'd have been soaked. Instead, he got to stand back and appreciate Ramon's yelp. It came out much more high-pitched than the larger man's frame had led Faiz to expect.

"Better hurry up, Ramon," he called from across the street to his teammate.

A quick staticky buzzing sounded in the earpiece Faiz wore under his balaclava, putting an immediate end to his teasing. He stuck fingers between his lips and produced a sharp, direct "stop you in your tracks" whistle. The crunch and slide of boots on gravel, his teammates halting mid-stride, echoed back to Faiz.

"What is it, Faiz?" Katya asked, her voice coming in loud and clear—like she was just another thought in his head.

"Got a survivor. Two blocks east."

"Okay," Katya said. "Lead the way. We'll follow."

"Roger."

Of course, Faiz knew *why* Katya wanted him to take point, why she'd selected him for the team in the first place. He couldn't deny his talent for tracking, for picking up subtle clues others often overlooked. It's why Katya kept him in the back—to catch what everyone else missed.

He navigated a course he hoped the others wouldn't find too convoluted. He waved a hand, parting clouds of black and white smoke in front of his nose.

This San Francisco smelled different from the city Faiz remembered. It stank of an unnatural clash of campfire ashes and noxious chemicals spewed into the sky from the remnants of factory smokestacks. It brought tears to his eyes.

The girl sat on the cracked remains of another former sidewalk corner. The curved half-moon of the indented curb made an island amid the new sea of asphalt chunks. She wore her hair in pigtails. Faiz thought her pink overalls and white jumper looked far too clean for the middle of a disaster zone. From his observation point, he watched her draw stick-figure pictures in the ashes with her fingertips.

Faiz gave the "Stop" signal to the others. When he glanced back to make sure they'd followed his command, he suppressed a yelp. Katya, having made her way from the rear, now stood by his side. The look she gave—so sharp, Faiz worried she'd draw blood—cut his gasp off in his throat.

She nudged him forward. Closer to the girl. The toe of a boot struck a chunk of cement, sending it spiraling across the wreckage. Headed for the girl.

She stopped drawing, standing up, right when the cement skidded across her canvas. She looked over at Faiz, Katya, and the others. *Why's she so calm?* Faiz couldn't help wondering.

Katya's palm slapped across his shoulder blade, returning him to reality.

"Piper, Maurice, go take a look at her!" she called to the others.

The other team members jumped into action. No hesitation or daydreaming on their parts.

The girl balanced on tiptoes, surveying her would-be rescuers. She didn't even look like she'd thought about running. Faiz chuckled to himself. The little girl's apparent bravery impressed, but also confused him.

"Here we are, end of the world, and this girl still trusts grown-ups like us. For all she knows, we're the cause of that damn dog destroying us all," he said.

"Transport's coming," Katya said, ignoring Faiz's commentary.

Faiz stayed by his boss's side, shadowing her while she moved among the other members of the team and dispensed additional orders.

He couldn't recall if they'd said how long it took for the city to fall in the briefing. But from the moment the simulation started, he'd sensed a world below the concrete, brick, and glass façade, a world in waiting. A world poised to take control again.

A rumble sounded from around the corner. A massive engine purred and tires ground up the shattered remnants of a world destroyed. Right on cue, the Evac Truck rolled across the exploded glass and plastic of a vandalized corner store ATM. Twenty-dollar bills were ground to confetti under tire treads.

Katya supervised Piper and Maurice's examination of the girl. Faiz couldn't help but notice how she kept her distance from the child. When the medics finished, Katya gave a satisfied nod. She turned to Faiz. "Look around," she said to him, "There's no one else but us."

He hadn't had a chance to raise his concerns about Katya calling in the Evac Truck before they'd found a single survivor. "But one girl. I mean is…"

She ignored him and instead gave Maurice the go-ahead to scoop up the girl and place her inside the truck. "One little girl *is* enough," Katya said. "She has to be."

*At the end of the day, she's in charge.* Faiz shrugged and climbed into the back of the truck, with the rest of his team. One spot remained by the back double doors at the end of one of the long benches stretching to the front cabin. Up there, Vana—the team's driver—revved the engine. She wouldn't stick around a second longer than necessary.

Faiz didn't blame her.

He looked down the benches on either side of the transport. Everybody looked as exhausted and overwhelmed as Faiz imagined himself to appear. His gaze settled on the girl.

Maurice had strapped her in tight. Her delicate feet, clad in open-toed white sandals, didn't reach the floor. They dangled, swinging back and forth.

Déjà vu gripped Faiz and squeezed for a long time. *I've seen her before.* With certainty settled in his guts, he knew it'd been somewhere other than the ruins of a major metropolitan city. Somewhere other than some made-up end of the world.

He hesitated, not quite ready to snap his safety harness straps in place. An unsettling familiarity compelled him to open his mouth one more time. "What's your name?" he asked the girl.

The Big Good Boy's mournful, desperate howl resounded through the wreckage before she could answer. The beast's drawn-out cry echoed off the remaining buildings. The team froze. Like a warren of rabbits ambushed by the hunt.

They all had a damn good idea what would happen next.

Of course, they weren't frozen long. They were pros. Vana's foot came down hard on the gas pedal. The truck shot forward, driven like a disoriented bear up too early from hibernation. Still not strapped in, Faiz fell from his perch. The way he fell, he barely missed getting his teeth knocked to the back of his throat.

"I'm okay! I'm okay!" he said, but no one listened.

He managed to pull himself into a crouch. His hand gripped the front edge of the bench.

Team members seated close enough to the front craned their necks forward. They all tried to get a glimpse past Vana's headrest, to peer through the windshield. Those seated further back contented themselves with muttered prayers to whatever gods might listen.

The Evac Truck fishtailed through more wreckage. Faiz checked where the girl was supposed to be sitting. But she wasn't there. She was standing on the shaking, rattling metal bench. Faiz didn't understand. He was sure he'd seen Maurice strap the girl in.

*No one's paying attention to her. I know we've got a giant creature heading our way, but dammit they have to see the more immediate danger right in front of their faces, right?*

Faiz got into a crouch and moved inch by inch down the aisle toward the standing girl.

When he got close enough, Faiz stood and took her hands in his own. He pulled her down, bringing her toward the edge of the bench. He tried to be gentle, but he also wanted to make sure she got the message loud and clear: being up and out of her seat at the moment was a bad idea. He buckled her harness, still not sure if it was being done for the first time or second. She held up a hand, her fingertips grazing his cheek. The sudden skin-on-skin contact sent a shiver through Faiz's body.

More sirens blared.

Then, Katya's hand dropped onto Faiz's shoulder. She pulled him back from the girl.

"Katya, I'm—"

Before he finished, Vana screamed. The Evac Truck surged forward on one last wild ride. Then, stopped.

Katya kept a tight grip on Faiz's shoulder to prevent him from flying through the windshield. But it wasn't enough to keep him upright. He fell across Piper's lap.

Faiz expected to be greeted with a scowl by the medic who'd turned him down for enough dates to the point where he thought he might qualify for a punch card, but when he looked up, Piper's face was blank. Just a pale empty canvas. Until he rubbed his eyes and there she was again—eyes, nose, mouth, the whole deal.

*Simulator must be fritzing*, he thought.

Relieved of her "saving Faiz" duties, Katya headed to the front. The girl appeared ready to stand and follow her. Her hands fumbled at the clasp on her harness. "Make sure she stays put," Katya called back to Faiz.

Running on instinct, he snapped off a quick, "Yessir."

"Vana, what's going on? Why aren't we moving?" Katya asked the driver.

Faiz pointed to the girl, then down to the bench, hoping he'd made it clear enough so the girl knew not to try and move again. Then, he stole a glance back at the doors through which they'd boarded the truck. He performed the calculations in his head, trying to figure out if he had the strength to shove open those doors and make a break for it before all hell broke loose.

The girl appeared resigned to fate. Faiz wondered why she still didn't cry or pray or perform some combination of the two acts.

"What do *you* think's going on out there?" he asked her.

The girl's eyes flashed upward but didn't stop at Faiz's face. Soon enough, she was looking past him. He followed her gaze, as it settled on the roof.

From outside the truck, the Big Good Boy growled and snarled. His vocalizations produced a deep, skin-penetrating sound. It traveled up through the soles of Faiz's feet and shook him so hard his teeth chattered. He dropped to his knees, clapped hands over his ears. Tears streamed unbidden from his eyes.

Katya abandoned Vana up front and headed back to Faiz and the girl. She struggled to move against the vibrations produced by the giant creature's yelps. "The g-g-g-g-girl..."

Katya fought for every syllable. Faiz tried to stand. This time, others joined him. Their restraints clicked off, one after the other. Those who had weapons access unholstered their pieces. Faiz didn't know what good they'd be against the beast waiting outside, towering above them and blocking the only way out of the city hellscape.

Something heavy fell onto the roof of the Evac Truck. A loud, frantic scratching followed. Worse than a chorus of ten thousand fingers on ten thousand chalkboards. The metal plating of the roof tore away like wrapping paper shredding. Faiz caught brief glimpses of the curled yellow claw-like nails springing from the black paw pads of the Big Good Boy.

Katya almost made it back to the girl. Close enough so she could've touched her. But she didn't.

Then, the roof collapsed down on them. Faiz threw his arms up in a final, meaningless, human gesture. A hunk of metal headed right for him.

Through the metal shower, in the final moments before the end, Faiz stared into the bloodshot eyes of the Big Good Boy. He didn't need a long look. He found no evil or malice in the creature's eyes.

*Looks more like he wants a friend.*

The giant dog snorted and snuffed, breathing in the musk, sweat, and fear of the NDPT.

People screamed.

Everything went dark.

"End scenario," Katya called. Even though he couldn't see her in the inky black oblivion at the end of the scenario, he was certain she rolled her eyes, disappointment radiating off her person.

***

The Big Good Boy, the girl, the Evac Truck, the blood, the wreckage, all those signs of a world gone wrong—they flashed and blinked themselves into oblivion. Like images spun through a disco-ball centrifuge. Faster. Faster. Pulse. Pulse.

Then—*poof*—they're gone.

Hands shaking, Faiz lifted the VR helmet off his head. He stepped away from his panel and left the helmet dangling like overripe fruit from its neuro-cables.

Faiz did a quick visual sweep of the Simulation Room. He knew there was nothing to worry about, but needed some concrete signifier to help him overcome the fear that gripped him.

He couldn't help it. He reacted the same way after every failed sim.

He let his hand brush against the gray-dyed foam walls. Trying to calm the world, his fingertips sank into the absorbent surface. The sensory-depriving material gave and gave at his touch.

The air in the Simulation Room tasted as Faiz expected it to—like nothing at all. No burning rubber. No acrid crackle at the back of his throat from standing too close to exposed and sizzling electrical wiring. No alarms and no surprises.

All the others—Ramon, Marcus, Vana, Piper—had already left. Faiz caught the closing door at the very last second.

He considered calling after his compatriots. But Faiz of the real world never displayed the confidence of Faiz in the simulations.

Then, from the back of the room, someone sniffled. A cry, swallowed back into someone's throat, followed. Faiz turned from the exit and found Katya, standing by the control booth and wiping away tears.

By the time Katya joined him at the exit, her face was clean. She'd assumed her usual stoic, dead-eyed "I'm the boss" mask worn as unassumingly as a thrift-store cardigan draped over the shoulders. "What was *that* all about?" Faiz asked her, positioning himself so he stood between Katya and the way out.

"That was today's scenario," she answered. "We run whatever scenario is assigned. And we use each unique iteration to help us prepare for potential disasters. It's the job. Remember?"

"Sure, sure," Faiz said, "But a giant *dog*? That's more like something out of an old sci-fi flick or something. Attack of the 50-Foot Rover!"

He didn't want to ask Katya about the giant dog—the "Big Good Boy" as the briefing materials had dubbed the creature. The Big Good Boy *was* absurd. An impossibility. But he also understood the Norbrid Disaster Preparedness Team experienced enough outlandish scenarios—from "flame-throwing terrorists during the aftermath of a tidal wave" to a "combination earthquake and locust swarm"—for the distinction not to matter.

He really wanted to ask Katya about the girl. After all, she didn't look or act like any of the other VR-generated "citizens" Faiz had ever encountered in the Simulation Room.

*Where did she come from? Who was she? Why'd she look at you, Katya—and you at her—like you knew each other?*

Something compelled Faiz to hold his questions, and as a result, they remained unanswered.

Sensing his hesitation, Katya slipped past. The exit door opened as her palm touched its smooth, sleek surface.

"You're not gonna tell me why we did *that* particular scenario?" Faiz asked, following her into the corridor.

"No, I'm not," Katya answered.

She marched on to her office, leaving Faiz to stand alone in the sterile, overly-lit corridor of the Norbrid Disaster Preparedness Center. After a while, he had nothing better to do than laugh.

***

Another day, another disaster. New loose and shattered pavement crunched under the treads of Faiz's boots. Vibrations from aftershocks traveled up his legs. Still, he kept his balance, hopping from one broken piece of earth to the next. He couldn't suppress the smile creeping over his face while he moved. After all, he loved this part of the job—so much like coming home, like visiting an old friend to reminisce about the glory days.

Faiz played his part to perfection. He executed every maneuver with a level of skill and efficiency achieved via hours and hours of practice. Already he'd helped set up the triage tent and then pivoted to tackling the removal of more manageable chunks of rubble from the entrance to the bank building—the one with the caved-in roof.

"Vana, pass me the light!" he shouted.

There she stood, right by his side.

"Ah damn!" Faiz flinched, as Vana held out the flashlight.

There was no spark of recognition in her eyes, only an impatient expression like the customers in the bank's long lines might've worn before the end of their world came. "Van, you okay?"

She pushed the light into his hand, insistent.

Faiz took the skinny black flashlight from her and directed its beam through the remains of the bank's crumpled gold-plated doors. *Gotta remember to compliment Katya on the detail*, he thought.

When he turned back to thank Vana, she was gone. Somehow, Faiz hadn't even heard the crunch of concrete accompanying her departure.

He finished dragging away the heavier chunks of the concrete archway and then stepped through the rubble-strewn entrance. His boots slid against pebble-sized shards of glass and he held an arm out for balance. Palms pressed flat against a cold marble slab—some art installation left behind in the bank's foyer.

Over the years, the verisimilitude of the disaster simulations led to over half the NDPT recruits washing out after only a few scenarios. Sometimes, the reactions were more extreme, with recruits running off screaming mid-simulation, followed by their avatars getting crushed by an AI-generated flying manhole cover. Or something worse. Some experienced a slow, identity-unraveling panic attack—their brain's rebellion against the impossible. Either way, neuro-tube feeds would get cut and those who couldn't hack it ended their day with a handshake, a referral to a relatively affordable therapist, and a "no hard feelings" final pay-o ff.

Faiz never had any of those problems. He'd taken to it with ease. Like he was born to it. He welcomed the challenge, the thrill from dipping in and out of these made-up ruined worlds.

He proceeded into what remained of the bank building. He was supposed to head to the vault—the one in which the bank employees huddled waiting for extraction.

But then, Faiz came around the corner and discovered—there wasn't any vault.

Instead, a large hole went through the marble-tiled, concrete-reinforced floor and revealed the ground below, turned like so much tilled soil. A sinkhole to Hell—it looked as though it went down deep enough at least.

The girl—the same girl from the previous day's "Big Good Boy" scenario—sat at the edge of the hole. Her restless legs dangled in the dark. She appeared to whisper something to whomever or whatever resided in the shadowy depths.

"Some help here?!" Faiz called into his headset.

Again, he began a slow approach toward the girl. His stomach grumbled, but he didn't know if it was a hunger "felt" in the simulation or in the real world.

In a flash, he experienced a feeling of dual existence, like he was looking down on himself in the scenario and back in the training room. He didn't understand. If he was outside both of those places...then where *was* he supposed to be?

A cold sweat broke across his brow. No one responded to his earlier query. It was unlike his teammates to leave a request for help unanswered.

Once he'd moved close enough to the girl where he could grab her if she spooked and tipped forward, Faiz cleared his throat.

She locked eyes with him. For all his precaution, it was Faiz who ended up stumbling. He dug his heels into the destroyed cement, halting his one-way ticket for a fall of Humpty-Dumpty proportions.

*He'd never been that athletic or dexterous before his work at Norbrid. But something about the work brought out new facets of his being.*

The girl remained seated, watching her would-be rescuer teeter on the edge of oblivion.

"I...I..." Words caught in Faiz's throat.

"Faiz! Get away from her!"

He fell back, away from the hole and the girl, as Katya stomped through the shattered ruins. She made a bee-line for Faiz and the girl.

Faiz took a quick glance into the hole. Good thing, too. With this split second of visual input, he managed to jump out of the way, avoiding the impact of the burnt sienna-colored furry paw bounding from the abyss. Then, another of the Big Good Boy's paws slapped at the rim of the hole. Its pads pressed against ruined tiles—inches from where Faiz had stood.

"Good God!"

He scurried back, moving further from the hole. It wasn't real. He *knew* it wasn't real. But it didn't change the sensation of churning dread bubbling within whatever his "real" self-thought of as his stomach in the simulated plane where he "existed."

Faiz watched the Big Good Boy pull his massive body out of the pit. Each of the gargantuan beast's breaths came as a brief blast with the intensity of gale-force winds. Like the one's encountered by Faiz and his co-workers in countless extreme weather simulations. The few remaining panes of glass in nearby buildings shattered, blowing pieces back inside. Faiz dug his feet into the destroyed ground, raised an arm to cover his face.

Then, hands gripped Faiz from behind. He turned to confront his savior. Faiz's five o'clock shadow rubbed against Katya's bodysuit. She pulled him away from the hole, unrelenting and single-minded in pursuit of her goal.

"But the girl!"

Faiz couldn't stand up to his supervisor's near limitless supply of energy though. He watched her put more and more daylight between them and the Big Good Boy. From a distance, the beast looked more like a storybook guardian towering over the girl than any monstrous threat.

The Big Good Boy stood up on its back paws, assuming the begging position of its much smaller kin. Front paws extended. One floppy ear hung over a tall, wet eye. The dark eye, reminded Faiz of those forbidden parts of the lakes by his parent's cabin—those spots they'd warn him and his brother to stay away from.

Katya put herself in front of Faiz, blocking his path back to the girl and the Big Good Boy. Faiz didn't understand what'd gone wrong with the scenario. He cycled through the names of their teammates. "Piper? Maurice? Vana? Karl? Rodriguez? Newman? Deena?" Some of the names he called were \ departed team members, but it didn't matter. The only response he got was silence. Not even the hiss of radio static from untended two-ways. Everyone was gone.

*But that didn't make sense. No one could leave unless the scenario ended. And Katya hadn't ended the scenario. So where were the others? Hadn't they heard? Hadn't they seen?*

"Dammit, aren't we going to save her?" he asked Katya.

Katya yelled her answer back over a rising crescendo of sirens and alarms. "No!"

"End simulation," Faiz said.

Katya shook her head. "Cancel order."

"End simulation," Faiz repeated, staring bullets back at Katya.

"Cancel order."

Faiz closed his eyes, and he let himself go.

*Remember, none of this is real.*

"Stop!"

Faiz didn't recognize the voice shouting the command. It wasn't from Katya or any of his missing teammates.

He opened his eyes and laughed at who he found waiting.

Not Katya. Not the girl. Not even the Big Good Boy. Though it wouldn't have shocked him if the creature moved its mouth to speak, black-and-pink gums and white teeth moving through each unnatural syllable.

Instead, he found a scared-looking, flop sweat-drenched beat cop with his service weapon drawn. He aimed the gun at Faiz's chest—center mass.

Faiz "recognized" the cop after a long look. "Officer Friendly" was what he and the others had dubbed the generic cop character designed by Katya and inserted into many of the previously-run scenarios.

"Stop!"

Faiz laughed again. He took in the sight before him: Officer Friendly with his finger on the trigger. A simulated finger belonging to a simulated man, inching closer and closer to the simulated trigger of a simulated gun. Faiz stifled the laughter, even though he didn't want to. After all, his laughter stood as the one genuine thing he had going for him.

"Please don't shoot," he said, "I'm a member of the Norbrid Disaster Preparedness Team."

*Like we practiced.*

"D-d-don't move!"

*Well, that didn't work.*

"Damn you, Katya."

Faiz hoped she heard him. He glanced past the frightened, not-real cop. Katya was heading back to the girl.

"What are you saying? What are you saying?" Officer Friendly wasn't giving Faiz time to answer.

"Come on, man," Faiz said, feeling ridiculous for trying to reason with a ghost in the machine. "Check the uniform. Read the company logo. Not to mention you've got *much* bigger things to worry about. Like the earthquake damage—and the giant dog standing up back there."

"Dog? What are you talking about?"

Faiz pointed over the false man's shoulder. "There! There! By the hole!"

"You're crazy." Officer Friendly wouldn't look.

"And you're not *real*."

The Big Good Boy barked.

Faiz took a step forward, moving on instinct toward the hole. Something pulled him to Katya, the girl, and the Big Good Boy. It wasn't a sense of danger or fear. With the giant monster puppy and the two blondes—almost the same hair color even—frozen in place like a fun-house mirror image of Americana before him, Faiz felt a smile sneaking in. He stayed focused on the tableau before him and missed when the explosion came, the bullet leaving Friendly's gun.

Lucky for him he didn't have to live with the memory of the bullet hitting his chest. The simulation was canceled and Faiz was thrown back to his real world.

***

Each breath taken while wearing his VR helmet echoed in Faiz's ears. When he took the helmet off, he was alone.

He made a fist and struck the padded walls. Back in the Simulation Room, there was no girl. There was no Big Good Boy. No wet dog fur and broken earth musk. With the simulation over, Faiz stood in a dark and empty room with the hum of dormant machinery all around him.

The others, minus Katya, waited in the locker room. They'd gathered into their usual packs. Faiz joined his cluster—Ramon, Vana, Marcus, and some of the others whose names he still hadn't learned. "Pretty wild, huh?"

Nobody responded. Like Faiz hadn't said anything at all.

He continued, undeterred. "I mean, the giant dog coming back. You know? And the girl? What do we even think *that's* about?"

"What are you talking about?" Marcus asked. The others' faces mirrored the confusion evident in Marcus's tone.

After everyone dressed, the others converged at the locker room door. Someone mentioned hitting "the bar." Someone Faiz didn't recognize—*and he thought he knew everyone on the team*—gave a side-long glance in his direction. But the others all shook their heads. They moved in a tight pack, shunning the outsider.

Faiz didn't follow. The way no one looked back again made it clear they were more than fine with his decision.

*I'm not hungry or thirsty anyway.* Faiz couldn't remember the last time he'd eaten or drank anything. But he didn't have time for new questions about his health and condition. There were older, bigger questions still lingering.

Faiz embarked on his search.

He was good at finding people, but this time would be different. This time, he'd have to put those skills to work in the mundane disaster of reality—where the world kept going and going, making it much harder to figure out how to play the hero.

After minutes crept into an hour and beyond, Faiz wasn't sure how many doors he'd opened, drawers he'd rifled through, file folders he'd laid open on desktops, or papers he'd flipped through. But for all his searching, he still didn't believe he'd found anything close to the answers he wanted.

He had narrowed his search to two rooms though. Katya's office *was* off-limits. Until it became impossible to avoid. But one last viable option still remained. In truth, Faiz wanted to kick himself for not zeroing in on it sooner.

Back where it'd all started, he stood in the Simulation Room. He bobbed and weaved between the empty VR helmets dripping from the neuro-cables' curved branches, leading back to the control booth—the source from which all the training scenarios fed.

He'd watched Katya activate the control booth panels countless times. He found it easy to copy his boss's movements, bringing up the "Scenario Prep Screen." Every file—every scenario—came numbered and named. Everything from 001 FOREST FIRE to 007 MASSIVE EARTHQUAKE to 025 STATUE OF LIBERTY TERRORIST AT-TACK, and so on. But one file bucked the naming convention, two words under the folder icon: "THE END."

Faiz set the controls to start the scenario. Then, he slipped on his helmet. As his eyes adjusted, he saw two very familiar faces.

***

"I'm so happy you tracked me down, Faiz," Katya said.

She leaned back in a reclining leather desk chair—a fancy one. Much fancier than Faiz could recall her ever using at work. This Katya appeared confident but in a relaxed, friendly manner. Nothing like the granite-carved badass who ran the Norbrid Disaster Preparedness Center.

"Oh, you know me. I'm good at finding people," Faiz said.

Except it wasn't Faiz who was speaking.

Of course, it looked like him. This other Faiz stood on the opposite side of the other Katya's desk. He dressed to the nines in designer clothing. No NDPT jumpsuit for him.

The original Faiz—the "real" Faiz—knew his body waited in the Simulation Room, standing stock still with a VR helmet over his head. The sights in front of him left him paralyzed with dread though. He stood in the doorway of a room he didn't recognize. But the moment unfolding before him felt familiar.

"Figured you'd find this eventually," Katya said.

There *she* was. The hard-edged, no-nonsense team leader. The "real" Katya that Faiz knew best. She stood at his side so both could look in on their other-selves. She rested her hand on Faiz's arm. It surprised him to find her touch so soft. Gentle. He wondered how different his Katya was from the other before them.

The other Faiz and the other Katya were as unaware of their door-way-dwelling doppelgangers' presence as Officer Friendly was of the Big Good Boy. Indeed, they'd kept up their separate conversation without a break. The other Katya spun around one of the flickering holo-screens above her desk so the other Faiz could get a better look. Her perfect nails pointed to certain items highlighted on the screen. The other Faiz leaned in. He appeared plenty interested in what the other Katya offered.

"You remember during our Norbrid days when I got you to volunteer for the brain-mapping project?" she asked

The other Faiz nodded. A slight, admiring grin turned the corners of his lips.

"The original data collection process was a bit roughshod. I didn't know what I was doing. I gathered everything. So, it took a while to refine and complete the mapping process. Started with pets first. That's how I got my initial funding. Sold it as a means of helping owners who wanted to keep their cats or dogs or whatever around after they'd passed on. But then, we made some breakthroughs in tech and more seed money came for human trials. And...we did it, Faiz."

The other Faiz didn't say anything. But he didn't need to. His face spoke volumes.

"The tech we've developed, it takes the data collected and maps your entire brain—every thought, every memory, every idea—good or bad, everything inside your head making you, well, *you*. And we load the other "you" to our secure environment. And then, well...

"Are you saying what I think you're saying, Katya?" the other Faiz asked.

Back in the doorway, Faiz's Katya tightened her grip on his arm.

"We place the copy of your consciousness—based on your brain as I recorded it back at Norbrid—into this dynamic environment…"

"But my body's gone?" the other Faiz interrupted.

Other Katya nodded. "What we upload's a snapshot. A moment in time. Your uploaded consciousness will continue to grow inside this environment. It'll learn, evolve, like the consciousness inside your body will continue to do out here. Until it expires, of course."

"I see," the other Faiz said.

"Since you're mapped, I can even go ahead and upload you now."

"Like now-now? Won't I get lonely if it's me in there?"

"No, no. We've developed some agile AI-controlled avatars. They're limited in terms of depth, but adaptable nonetheless. And, besides, you weren't the only one who got their brains scanned back in the Norbrid days…"

Realization dawned across the other Faiz's face. "*You?* You're telling me you uploaded yourself?"

"Of course. The other me's waiting for you."

"Doing what? What're we supposed to do in there?"

"I decided to go with what she'd—what we'd find familiar. And exciting, too. I've got her supervising VR disaster prep work. Back in those Norbrid days, I was always work-work-work, y'know? I thought my other-me might appreciate it."

The other Faiz chuckled. "You were a real pain in the ass back then," he said.

"It's from before I met Mark. Before, we had…well you know. I don't believe the old me would recognize the me of today."

The other Faiz reached across the desk and took the other Katya's hand in his. Friends connecting in celebration. "Of course, she would," he said, "She became you after all."

"Okay," he said, once they'd let go of each other's hands, "Let's do it."

From a keyboard at her desk, the other Katya pressed buttons—and then: "It's done," she said.

"Like that?" the other Faiz asked.

"Like—"

Alarm bells and sirens rang out, all around and inside the building. Those elements put Faiz at ease, making the unfolding scene more familiar. The impending chimes of disaster—a tune he'd grown accustomed to.

"Oh my God, what happened to New York..." Snippets of sob-choked conversation leaked in from outside the other Katya's office. She turned around another of the many holo-screens, directing it to a news channel.

Faiz heard plenty. Reports came in, delivered by anchors drowning in a waking nightmare. "Coordinated attacks...dirty bombs...nuclear launch..."

The other Katya tried to stand up from behind her desk, but the trembling and sobs shaking her were obvious even to Faiz watching from outside the room. Meanwhile his counterpart hurried to the other Katya's side, taking her hand and easing her back toward the desk.

"I must go," she said, trying to push past the other Faiz, but also not putting up much of a fight either. "The nanny was running late. And I got so busy this morning, I never called to confirm she'd made it. I left my Parental Drone following my babygirl though. I told myself it wouldn't be long. It'd let me know if anything happened. It's not like *no one's* watching her. And besides, there's the dog…"

Faiz couldn't take anymore. He couldn't watch and do nothing.

He took a step forward, meaning to cross the threshold. But some invisible force bounced him back.

Again, his presence outside the office went unnoticed. Other Katya embraced the other Faiz, both standing there in the middle of the room. Faiz soon figured out the whistling wasn't in his head. It was "real"—as real as possible.

He caught a final split-second glimpse inside. Everything went bright white. His Katya covered his eyes and her words followed in a choked whisper.

"We—the other you and other me—died after the bombs fell. I don't know how much time passed…out there. I'm not even sure how the footage got uploaded into our scenario. Knowing me, I automated it in case of an emergency and had it stored off-site. Somewhere. It took me a long time to find it. But I'm not sure. Could've been no time at all."

She pulled her hands back. Faiz looked inside a solid wall of black, a wall of nothing at all. He turned and found nothing more than nothing behind them as well. Everywhere he looked—up, down, side to side—unfathomable emptiness. *At least I'm not alone*, he thought.

"If everything's true—*if*, then it means we're…"

Katya nodded in reply.

"Yes. You and I—we've always lived in disaster."

"Cancel this scenario, Katya," Faiz said. His words emerged in a hoarse, rasping growl.

*But there is no growl. I'm not HEARING anything. There's no "me" to hear or to be heard. And there's not even a "me" back in the Simulation—*

Real or not, Faiz found himself back in the Simulation Room. He didn't take off his helmet, so much as he fell from it, crumpling to the ground and wrapping his arms around his knees. When he looked up at the walls and the ceiling, everything appeared degraded to black nothingness.

*There aren't any walls. No control booth, no helmets, no me.*

He looked at his hands. He'd never thought much about his hands. They *were*. And they were *his*. But examining them in the moment, he didn't find the scratches, moles, wrinkles, and far too many knuckle hairs—those he'd neglected hundreds, thousands, even millions of times before.

Not to say those features were gone. Faiz simply viewed them in a new light. They appeared as numbers—repeating sequences—lines of code. The code behind his so-called existence.

*I'm not real. I'm not real. I'm not real.*

"I'm not real," Faiz said the words out loud. Even his voice sounded false to ears he no longer trusted.

He didn't get to speak again. Didn't get to unravel further. Katya's slap across his face ended any thought of disintegration.

It didn't matter whether the slap was "real" or not. It hurt like hell. Faiz groaned. He held his palm against the growing ache of his cheek.

"Pull yourself together," she said. It didn't sound like one of her orders though. Instead, she was begging him.

She was crying.

The pieces fell into place.

"The girl...she's your..."

***

"...your daughter." As Faiz finished his sentence, the briefing room's carpeted floor gave way under his feet. They'd shifted scenarios—without the control booth, without the helmets.

*I guess we never needed them.*

Katya nodded. Then, shook her head. "Yes. No. I mean..."

Faiz stepped back and waited for her full answer to come.

"I—I mean—the other Katya, the flesh and blood one, she had a daughter years after she got scanned. After I was created or whatever you want to call it. I wouldn't even know about the girl if I'd never found the file. If I never looked, I would've never known I...she...had a—"

"Come here," Faiz said. A day before, even a half-hour before, he wouldn't have imagined it, but he held his arms open and waited for Katya to step into his embrace.

Her sobs overlapped with the thud of his beating heart.

Time passed, enough for Katya's tears to run dry at last. She pulled back. Faiz watched her, wiping under her eyes until the lower lids were left red and puffy. "I want to show you something else," she said.

Again, the room fell away—ceiling, floor, walls, everything. All gone. But Faiz was ready for the change. With the details of the "world" stripped away, icons popped up before them—3D projections of different scenarios.

Faiz took in the "real" world—the outside. A city in ash. Everything reduced to rubble—a sandcastle ruined at the water's edge after the inevitable visit of crashing saltwater waves.

"After I found the first file, I needed to know more. About the end. It took some sleepless nights—or what we perceived as sleepless nights—but I found a way to access data from outside the parameters of whatever the "this" is that the other Katya set for us."

Faiz nodded along. At the same time, he knew science existed far beyond his comprehension.

*All that matters is I'm here and she's here.*

"It's easy once you get the hang of it. It's a matter of perspective, thinking of yourself as a bunch of code—instead of a person. I learned how to pull other security footage from the other Katya's office. Of course, she—*I* never brought the girl into work. I guess she wanted to keep her family and work separated? I don't know. It's what I would've done. So, I expanded my search..."

Another image expanded in front of Faiz. Satellite video footage—a destroyed upscale suburban neighborhood. Wiped almost flat by a nuclear blast. Open-floor plan ranch-style houses appearing as giant decapitated stumps in a black and soupy sea of melted asphalt.

One detail caught Faiz's eye amid the devastation. He leaned forward, sticking his head inside the image. He studied the black figures. They were the shadows of two once-living beings—caught near enough to the blast so their shades left a permanent mark across the remaining landscape. Faiz knew who they belonged to.

The first one was easy—it belonged to a little girl. A little girl who sat home alone when the sirens squawked to life. She must have wandered outside because she didn't know what else to do. So, she went calling for her Mama. But the other shadow took some time to figure out. It was so massive after all. It must've been caught *just so*, resulting in its stretching out above the girl's forever etched shade.

A dog's giant shadow.

"Good boy," Faiz said.

The tears coming from his eyes surprised Faiz. He'd experienced the aftermaths of enough disasters, all those potential end-of-the-world scenarios run time after time. He thought he'd buried any possible pain away. But then he witnessed the true end of the real world through the shadows of a lost little girl and her loyal dog. Faiz experienced the difference as hot razors dragged across tear ducts.

"I accessed the last uploaded files from the drone—since it linked back to Katya's office. These were the materials I worked with. I filled in what I could. I'm still not sure why. I thought it'd be enough to save her—once. But I couldn't leave it."

Faiz and Katya found themselves returning to the same broken street corner from the "Big Good Boy" scenario. From their new state of understanding, they stood back and watched everything play out before them. The scenario resumed from the point where Katya ordered the others to take the girl and load her into the Evac Truck. The Big Good Boy came bounding through the rubble, stumbling over the remaining buildings which served as obstacles for his rendezvous with the truck.

"What went wrong?" Faiz asked.

"I'm not sure," Katya said, "I don't know if something...someone should be able to add elements from inside a scenario—even to a tiny simulated reality inside a larger simulated reality like we're in now. The other-me didn't have a chance to finalize the safeguards against it though. Still, the system recognizes *something's* wrong. Something's inside it that doesn't belong."

Katya waved her hand again, returning them to black. "Everything's breaking apart," she said.

Faiz understood. No matter how hard he tried, he couldn't remember the names of their AI-generated teammates. Their faces came as blurs.

"What's happening?" he asked. He grabbed onto Katya, the last "real" person he knew. She didn't pull away.

"The system's trying to purge rogue elements, but there's no one else out...there to manage it. So, it's shutting *everything* down. You noticed the change with the bank vault. The rest of team?"

Faiz nodded. Even the team they'd gone on the original Big Good Boy mission had been smaller than on any of the previous practice runs. But he'd let it slide. When he considered it though, even letting things slide like that seemed out of character.

*How'd the world get smaller and smaller without me noticing?*

"The end of the world as we know it," he said, humming the old song to himself.

Surrounded by the formless darkness, Katya recreated a version of her counterpart's fancy desk chair and sank into its generous leather surface.

"Well," Faiz said, once she'd gotten settled, "What do we do now?"

Katya slumped low in the chair. She stared at her feet, with her shoulders hunched. "I don't know," she answered. "Maybe, we wait until everything's gone. Until we're gone."

Faiz considered turning away and screaming into the abyss.

*But what good will it do. We're already in it after all.*

Instead, he focused on the new Katya, the one seated before him. A defeated and despairing iteration.

He couldn't reconcile her with the woman he knew—in so many hopeless situations.

Faiz knew a Katya who'd built a world. He knew another Katya who got left behind in a made-up world, but who went on to build and rebuild—saving countless smaller worlds inside. Even facing the end, Faiz remained in awe of her abilities as a builder.

But when he thought some more about the past they shared, Faiz recalled what *his* thing was—and knew what needed to happen before the end.

"Teach me how it's done," he said.

"What?"

"Show me how to do it," he repeated. "Show me how you gathered the files. Teach me how to do it."

It took more coaxing beyond his initial request. But eventually, Katya agreed. "What's it matter one way or another?" she asked more than once. But when their "bodies" returned to the Norbrid Disaster Preparedness Center, Katya showed Faiz how she'd transformed her "body" into component data and journeyed past the safety of the world the other Katya made for them.

"It's not an exact science," she told him. "In certain respects, it works...because it works."

Faiz nodded along. He'd never considered himself a religious man. "But there's comfort in the uncertainty."

Katya smiled despite herself. "Then, you're ready," she said.

She reached out and grabbed Faiz's arm before he moved. Pulled him close. "Where're you going?"

Faiz was already engaged in the process, so his answer came like a faded recording—an echo from the dying. "Into the California State Pet Registration Database..."

***

Katya looked at her hands. All alone.

And hating it.

*I should let myself go completely. Unravel and end it all.*

But she couldn't bring herself to do it. Not yet at least.

She looked up and studied the ceiling of the Norbrid Disaster Preparedness Center. At first glance, it appeared the same as she'd always remembered it.

But when she looked closer, she picked out the cracks—the splits in the seams of a disintegrating reality. The walls, the ceiling, and even the floor beneath her chair disappeared. This time forever.

She spent so much time focused on what wasn't there, she didn't notice their return at first. But the sandpaper roughness and sweet, hot breath against her knuckles brought her focus back.

She reached down and scooped up the dog—*their* dog. He embraced her in a way the other Katya had doubtless grown accustomed to before her world ended.

The dog's front paws draped over Katya's shoulders. He covered her in sloppy tongue kisses. On her cheeks and the insides of her ears. Even across her eyelids. He left not an inch untouched.

Katya stroked her hand through the dog's fur. "Good boy."

She looked past the not-so-big good boy squirming in her arms. Faiz followed.

He wasn't alone.

The girl peered from behind his legs. Her skin, hair, and eyes were a motley of blues and yellows and grays.

The way a dog remembered a person he loved.

"Told you I'm good at finding people," Faiz said. "Turns out I'm also good at finding dogs. Good thing you uploaded pets first, huh?"

Katya set the dog on the ground. Before doing so, she made sure to plant a smooch of her own on his wet nose. The girl stepped from behind Faiz. Then, she ran into her mother's arms. She called Katya

"Mama," and the way her speech trembled like a murmur, a re-creation of human speech as filtered through the canine ear, didn't matter.

Katya didn't care. Perfection belonged to simulated worlds. What Katya held in her arms was as real as she could ever want.

"Thank you."

Faiz nodded his "You're welcome" back to her.

He looked at the dog panting by his leg. Something rested in the mutt's mouth. Fuzzy and round. A tennis ball. *Of course.*

The dog wagged his tail. Thumped it against the ground.

Faiz smiled. He pulled the ball out of the dog's mouth. The creature "fought" for a moment, but gave up quick enough. Faiz cocked his arm. Then, he threw the ball as hard as he could. The dog ran under the arcing path of the ball.

As he ran, the last of the Norbrid Disaster Preparedness Center melted away. One last reset onto an expansive green landscape—comprised of lush and rolling hills. A tiny farmhouse sitting at the end of a gravel driveway. *A good place for a dog.* Faiz and Katya beamed at each other, unaware of their shared conclusion.

"Her name's Mia," Faiz said, pointing to the girl whose hair Katya had already pulled into pigtails. Katya nodded. But she didn't need to be told. Deep inside—she already knew.

*Woof. Woof. Woof.*

With the ball gripped between its teeth, their dog bounded back to the trio. He'd gone so far to fetch it. And, as he came closer, he grew and grew and grew.

The little girl—the one named Mia—looked out at her approaching dog. And as he made the last leap into her waiting arms, he looked like a giant.

# The Children's Horror (cont'd)

I don't recall if I nudged Ms. Nina first or if she nudged me. But at a certain point, we pulled each other from the fog. We'd descended into a stupor on account of what the children's television showed us.

*No, not the television. The horror—the children's horror made all of this.*

Images fled from my brain like I'd turned on a basement light and sent spiders and cockroaches scurrying to dark recessed corners. *Dogs in people suits, children in masks, monsters from nightmares, and dream women by the sea. The end of the world and the onset of new, awe-inspiring visions.* Tears stained my cheeks and my heart beat as though it'd propel itself from my chest.

The way Ms. Nina rubbed her knuckles under her eyes made me suspect the programming had a similar effect on her. But then, she pointed out how the children were affected. Each small face frozen, awash in the glow of the TV screen. Indeed, the light's reach had grown since the shows' commencement, sending tendrils of illumination across the auditorium. We looked at the children, spotting thin lines of drool leaking from their mouths.

I hated the way my body and mind responded to this sight. No concern for their well-being, no desire to rush to their aid and make sure they were okay. Instead, I turned and looked to the double doors leading out of the auditorium. Ms. Nina's hand closed around mine. A firm grip.

She nodded, giving me the signal. I shuffled out of the back row, trying my best to avoid contact with the armrests or the seatbacks of the row in front of us. I willed my heels to stay quiet on the carpeted floor. Ms. Nina followed.

I pulled the door open. Ms. Nina came too.

*Where are you go—*

Once we made it out into the hallway, we pushed our bodies against the doors. As though it'd serve to keep them back.

A moment passed, then another. No sounds from inside the auditorium, no force pushing against the doors.

As one, we stepped away from the auditorium entrance.

"We've got to get out of here," I said.

***

I put my hand on Ms. Nina's shoulder and press my forehead to hers. "You don't believe we're going to get away from here that easy?" I say. I cock my head toward the open back door. If we step out here, it should lead to the playground. But I have my doubts. Nothing I've observed from the children's horror leads me to believe this'll end in any way but in tears.

She lifts her chin, regarding me with a cool side-eye. Like there was hope for me yet. *You're starting to sound like me, kid?*

"Who you callin'..."

I stumble back from the door when I realize Ms. Nina's lips haven't moved. Her hands reach to the top of her head. She pulls once, twice. The Ms. Nina skin comes away like the peel of a rotten banana, pooling at the tiny Reebok sneaker-covered feet of one of my children.

They're stacked one on top of the other, like kids in a trench coat trying to sneak into an R-rated movie, like you'd see in the cartoons. Except there are too many children to fit inside Ms. Nina's skin. Too many to fit inside the school.

They tower over me. A wobbly stack of children, lips chapped and sticky, eyes wide regarding me with the malicious curiosity of a child holding a magnifying glass on a single ant.

They still keep the door open though.

That part I didn't expect.

I'm not willing to wait and find out what's next. I stumble through the open door. Praying for sand and for sunlight reflected off the mirrored surface of the slide. Monkey bars, seesaws, all the trappings.

***

The cool air conditioning of the auditorium strikes my face here on the other side of the door. I reach a hand forward, touching the glass. A spark of static shocks me. My eyes widen. Through the glass of the television set, I watch the children file back into their seats. Hundreds, thousands, millions, and then one.

*"Again,"* they say. *"Let's watch them again."*

# THE ANTI-VIEWING GUIDE

**Note: Some spoilers for stories in the collection may follow. Read at your own risk!**

**The Children's Horror**

The title of this framing story comes from "The Children's Hour," a play by Lillian Hellman about headmistresses at a boarding school accused of having a lesbian affair. First learned about the play via "Ernest & Bertram," a short film with knock-offs satire with the two Sesame Street characters you can probably guess playing the lead roles.

In elementary school, when standardized testing was administered, one half of the students were brought to the auditorium and shown cartoons while the other half of classmates filled out Scantron sheets with number 2 pencils. On one occasion, I remember being shown this wild "Just Say No" crossover cartoon that has played no small part in the inspiration behind these tales. Have you really lived if Papa Smurf hasn't told you not to smoke crack?

Whatever you do, *don't* watch "Cartoon All-Stars to the Rescue."

### The Final Choice of Peter Chu

I like stories that involve exes of any kind. Lovers, friends, family. Former good or bad relationships. There's something so compelling about the tension that this shared history can create. In this case, where we're talking about a massive imbalance in the power dynamic and the protagonist putting his body through some fairly horrific changes to appear equal, I thought there was potential for some real tension and conflict throughout the story.

Additionally, "Billy" and "Kit" (Kid) are absolutely a play on the similarly Wild West Outlaw-named "Jesse" and "James."

Whatever you do, *don't* watch *Pokémon* in its approximately 1 bazillion incarnations.

### The Dogcatcher

I always feel bad for the hapless comedic villain on children's shows. Particularly with those shows aimed at a younger slice of the demographic, the bad guy's or gal's plots are typically as effective as a paper umbrella in a monsoon. And yet they become so intrinsically linked with the so-called heroes that you can't imagine the good guys, gals, or animal pals existing without their bumbling foils. With this particular story, the co-existence is taken to its unnatural conclusion.

Whatever you do, *don't* watch *Paw Patrol*.

### The Secret Society of Schrödinger's Children

With this story, I wanted to give it the feeling of one part of a larger story, the first episode of a serialized narrative. Comics like Grant Morrison's *Doom Patrol* and *Umbrella Academy* by Gerard Way and Gabriel Bá also played a significant part in the inspiration for this story.

That said, the main spark of an idea for the story came from a certain kids' show where the crime-fighting kid superheroes are always out late at night and I couldn't help wondering "Where the heck are their parents when all this is happening?"

Whatever you do, *don't* watch *PJ Masks*.

## Two Rare Specimens

"The Boogeyman" by Stephen King (from his *Night Shift* collection) has to be one of the scariest short stories I've ever read, with a protagonist who's an absolute piece-of-shit bastard. After reading that story, I slept with my closet door closed for a long, long time. In writing this story about siblings who are not as purely intentioned as they first seem, King's tale definitely had a role to play as far as inspiration goes.

I love stories where monsters aren't necessarily the villains. King's contemporary Clive Barker probably plays a not-so-small role on that front. Getting to play with the Boogeyman and the Monster Under the Bed as archetypal horrors was a lot of fun.

Whatever you do, *don't* watch *Wild Kratts*.

## The Shark in Her Belly

Several sibling stories feature in the collection, which feels like a natural fit. I grew up the oldest of three. Having brothers and sisters is a whole different type of horror story sometimes. But there can also be some real moments of connection that can't be duplicated outside of the sibling dynamic. This story ends with a relationship that I hope trends more to the positive (even though it's preceded by a lot of blood-shed and shark chomping).

Whatever you do, *don't* watch "Baby Shark" videos on YouTube.

**Your Selkie Lover**

Somehow, I ended up with back-to-back magical aquatic creature story. This one is a lot less gory, though it ramps up the eroticism. Unexpected inspiration source for this piece? *Diabolique*.

With this story, I wasn't aiming for horror exactly. More erotic literary slipstream. Which sounds like the most pretentious subgenre classification I could ever conceive. Which just means I'll have to try harder next time to conceive of something *more* pretentious. I also really wanted to write a selkie story.

Whatever you do, *don't* watch *My Little Pony: Friendship is Magic*.

**The Middle Sister's New Situation**

This story is one that's probably been with me the longest from this particular collection. Having grown up in the heyday of family sitcoms (1980s and 1990s with plenty of reruns in syndication and Nick at Nite from previous decades), it's a milieu I feel quite comfortable in exploring.

I remember an entertainment news story about one of the actors who played a daughter on one of those TGIF sitcoms who got into adult filmmaking after their character was written off. The adult film-making side seemed far less upsetting than this idea of someone being a part of a family one moment and then *poof* it's as if they never existed.

Earlier incarnations of the story featured the written-off daughter still in the sitcom world but exiled, unrecognized by their loved ones. Kind of an *It's a Wonderful Life* take. But I could never make it work. Having the character in the "real-world" and trying to adjust to her fictional status seemed to work a lot better.

Like "The Secret Society of Schrödinger's Children", this story is another concept that I'd be willing to revisit/explore further some time down the road.

Whatever you do, *don't* watch reruns of TGIF sitcoms from the 1990s.

## Rat Suit King

This story's origins exist at the cross-section of two very New York stories, both taken from around the seven or so years I spent living there after college. First: the stories of panhandlers dressed in mascot costumes, particularly those around Times Square. One such character dressed as the beloved Sesame Street character Elmo received a great deal of press and publicity, none of it positive, when they would attack and harass tourists and other bystanders.

The second much quieter and more mysterious NYC story involved the "Sad Panda," an individual who busked in a panda suit in the Financial District in the late 2000s. The character received a great deal of attention from the early Tumblr set and from *Gothamist*. Thinking about this individual wearing a panda costume and having strangers obsess and theorize over their existence struck me as an incredibly surreal bit of business.

And, toss in a certain world-renowned mouse character filtered through the ever-present rat population in the Big Apple and you've got yourself a "Rat Suit King."

There's also more than a little bit of my more self-destructive twenty-something incarnation from my early days in New York.

Whatever you do, *don't* watch people dressed up in animal mascot costumes or watch cartoons featuring M-I-C-K-E...you know what I'd rather not get sued so I'll just stop right there.

**The Big Good Boy**

The longest story in the collection and another attempt by yours truly to break my readers' hearts with giant monsters. Though, I'd hardly call *The Big Good Boy* of this story a monster, just a dog trying to take care of his person no matter what realm of existence or consciousness they find themselves in.

I've had the idea for a disaster preparedness team using virtual reality to train for various cataclysmic events and the line "We have always lived in disaster" (apologies to Shirley Jackson); but it was the introduction of the giant dog into the tale that brought the narrative together. This marks the second of my giant monster/American kaiju tales with the previous effort seen in my novella *Gargantuana's Ghost* from Grey Matter Press (available now!).

As someone who wept like a newborn after watching *Where the Red Fern Grows* in elementary school, if I can do my part to create a story where the dog somehow both dies *and* lives forever with his people, that's just what I am going to do.

Also, if you caught that Norbrid is a reference to Norman Bridwell, children's book author and illustrator, well, kudos to you.

Whatever you do, *don't* watch *Clifford the Big Red Dog*.


Actually, watch whatever you want. Watch whatever your kids (or whatever kids happen to be in your life) want. Have fun experiencing stories with them. Listen to the wild, weird worlds they make up and encourage them to keep doing so each and every day of their lives.

# ACKNOWLEDGEMENTS

This project started as an effort to translate all of the kids' TV programming my two children were watching during the height of the pandemic/lockdown here in Minnesota, USA through the filter of the weird, strange, and surreal, as it informs so much of my own writing. As a result, this book wouldn't possibly exist without Grant and Avery. Thanks, boys. This is all your fault.

On the other side of the equation, thanks also to my parents for fostering my love of writing and reading. Thanks also to them for indulging my many elaborate childhood fantasies about the cartoon characters *I* was obsessed with. This is also your fault.

Thanks to beta readers for many early incarnations of these stories—both those published previously and those getting their moment in the spotlight now. Thanks to J.V. Gachs, Christopher O'Halloran, Rachel Searcey, and Michelle Tang for your eyes and insights on these tales. They wouldn't be what they are now without you.

Thanks to Clay McLeod Chapman for his effusive, propulsive, and explosive foreword. Clay is a gentleman and a scholar. And if you haven't seen him do a live reading of his work, then you're missing out. Ask nicely and maybe he'll perform this stellar intro piece.

Thanks to Dan Howarth for your writing friendship and for taking a chance on this certainly rather strange concept for a short-story collection. Working with talented writers is always a plus for me because it helps one elevate their work to match the talent of their collaborators. You've certainly pushed me to raise the bar here, my friend. Cheers!

And, finally, thanks to Jenna. Thanks for your support, your patience, and your everything.

# ABOUT THE AUTHOR

Patrick Barb is an author of weird, dark, and horrifying tales, currently living (and trying not to freeze to death) in Saint Paul, Minnesota. His published works include the dark fiction collection *Pre-Approved for Haunting* (Keylight Books), the novellas *Gargantuana's Ghost* (Grey Matter Press) and *Turn* (Alien Buddha Press), as well as the novelette *Helicopter Parenting in the Age of Drone Warfare* (Spooky House Press). Visit him at patrickbarb.com.

# Also from Northern Republic

*Lionhearts*

by Dan Howarth

(coming 2024)

A politically charged thriller about class, hatred, and second chances. *The Lionhearts show their teeth when they smile, they can't wait to sink them into your flesh...*

Henry Oswald descends into desperation and the clutches of a local far-right group, the Lionhearts. Promised the world in exchange for his principles, he tries to pull himself free, only for their true nature to become ominously clear.

Henry's world is blown apart in an ill-fated insurance scam by a local Polish businessman, leaving him homeless and alone. Down and out, he meets Kelly, who helps him to believe that his life is worth something again as he bonds with her and her son. Henry is offered a hand by a local community scheme who use his story as a front for their own insidious aims in the community. Angry and fuelled by lies, Henry trades his principles for power and security. But the Lionhearts' web of violence can only reach so far and when Henry discovers the truth about them, answers won't be enough.

*Society Place*
by Andrew David Barker
(Out Now)

Set during the blazing English summer of 1976, recently widowed Heather Lowes moves into the house she was supposed to live with her husband.

But now she is alone.

Or at least, she thinks she is.

It is a normal terrace house, on an everyday, run-down working class street in a dying industrial town. A place that seldom sees the extraordinary.

However, when Heather meets her new neighbours – the old woman next door, the kid from a few doors down – they all seem concerned that she has moved into the house at the end of Society Place. They seem to know something.

Heather's nights in the house are troubled. She senses a presence, particularly on the stairs, and down in the cellar. She dare not go down there. As the sweltering summer rages on, Heather experiences supernatural turmoil that tests her sanity and pushes her understanding of reality to its very limits.

She learns that there isn't just one ghost.

There is a Nest of Ghosts that haunt, not just her house, but all the houses on Society Place. She also comes to learn of the Nest's interest in the baby growing inside her, and of the far-reaching consequences of the events of that summer and how they will still be felt into the first decades of the 21st century.